3/24

WATCH WHERE THEY HIDE

Also by Tamron Hall

As the Wicked Watch

WATCH WHERE THEY HIDE

A JORDAN MANNING NOVEL

TAMRON HALL

WITH T. SHAWN TAYLOR

WILLIAM MORROW
An Imprint of HarperCollins*Publishers*

WATCH WHERE THEY HIDE. Copyright © 2024 by Tamron Hall. All rights reserved. Printed in the United States of America. No part of this book may be used or reproduced in any manner whatsoever without written permission except in the case of brief quotations embodied in critical articles and reviews. For information, address HarperCollins Publishers, 195 Broadway, New York, NY 10007.

HarperCollins books may be purchased for educational, business, or sales promotional use. For information, please email the Special Markets Department at SPsales@harpercollins.com.

FIRST EDITION

Designed by Michele Cameron
Photo Credit: Shutterstock/AkimD

Library of Congress Cataloging-in-Publication Data has been applied for.

ISBN 978-0-06-303708-3

24 25 26 27 28 LBC 5 4 3 2 1

To the domestic violence hotline teams everywhere. You pick up the phone calls of strangers looking for someone to care like family, you hear the cries for help, and yet under the weight you never give up.

To the teams at Day One and Safe Horizon, you reminded me to listen with an open heart and use my voice for those who need me most.

1

Thursday, February 5, 2009

"Jordan? Jordan. If you would, please, follow me. Watch your step. Be careful. It's not well lit."

The massive warehouse in the heart of the former meatpacking district was still cold enough to hang meat even though Squalli and Sons had long ago shuttered its doors, leaving workers who had labored long, thankless hours to supply steaks and chops to some of Chicago's best restaurants to find new work, if they could get it.

"Okay, stop here," the raspy voice ordered.

My toes lined up exactly in the middle of the yellow tape pressed onto the bumpy cement floor. "Is this it?" I asked.

"Yes. Don't move."

I noticed some people in the crowd gazing up from their tasks to watch me awkwardly try and adjust to the right spot.

"Close your eyes for a sec." A whiff of air blew across my forehead as the bristles of a brush floated down to my nose.

"Ah! You moved," said the man, even more animated and antsy as he placed his body between me and the makeup artist. "Jordan, take a tiny step to the left. Good. This is the perfect spot to get the best camera angle. Don't move."

Don't move?

I could tell, four hours into my Justice Jordan promo shoot, the director's patience with multiple wardrobe changes—that jacket, but not this lipstick; a camisole versus a button-down blouse—had him fidgeting and anxious to get started. Ellen Holbrook, my assistant news editor, assured me this promotional campaign would catapult me and the investigative unit to the next level.

"A promo like this is a big, big deal, Jordan," she said. "You know there are no favors in this business. You're the lead investigative crime reporter now. The A1. You've covered some of the biggest stories in the city. You've earned it!"

Ellen proved herself to be the ultimate hype person at the shoot, hovering around to cheer me on and keep the nervousness from showing on my face. The camera catches it all. There's no hiding from the lens; it doesn't lie. When she wasn't poring over every line of the script, she was going back and forth to the two long folding tables piled high with assorted pastries, sandwiches and cheeses, a massive crab salad, and a chicken pasta that would be perfect to pack up for dinner tonight. Clark Catering, a local female-owned business, was just featured on our Best of Chicago segment and didn't disappoint. Someone even brought a legendary Eli's cheesecake. I bet it was Ellen. She knows it's my weakness.

In my four years at Channel 8, Ellen and I have formed somewhat of a sisterly bond. She was just as likely to critique my work as that of anyone else at the station, but she never tore me down to bring me down. She was a straight shooter with me and other women in the building, a good leader. But with those of us on the air, she didn't mince words. The extra scrutiny female talent has to put up with can be cruel and downright demoralizing in a way I think people don't fully grasp.

I caught my reflection in a full-length mirror. I definitely made the right choice, wearing a sheath dress with a strong blazer, the perfect balance of femininity and business. "It's like a fashion mullet. The dress is the party in the front, the jacket, the business in the back," I explained to Ellen, who was thoroughly amused, which is saying a lot for her. I've noticed when other people are around, she goes into her own code-switch mode and tries to present herself a certain way.

"Hey, Jordan. Look at these." The photographer hired for the shoot switched on his camera's LCD screen and shared some candids. He had been trailing me all afternoon but noticeably steered clear of the director, who was prepared to put up with my being indecisive and visibly uncomfortable with all of this, but that courtesy was not extended to others.

"Just a few more, Jordan. Can you look over here?" the photographer asked. "Turn just a little more toward me. Smile. Hold it."

This level of investment by the station came with a price. The yellow gaffer tape, the exact hue of crime scene tape, could mark the spot where my career died, too, if this campaign didn't spike ratings or bring Channel 8 enough attention to win a local Emmy.

"Where did you just go, Jordan?" the director sharply asked, snapping his fingers in my line of sight. "Come back."

"Sorry, Raphie."

The director's name was Raphael Navarro, but after this long day, I felt we were close enough to give him a nickname.

"I can't believe all of this is happening. It's been crazy."

"All the attention?" he replied, confused.

"Yes. The attention, the expectations. It's a lot."

Raphie was perplexed. He was used to people being thrilled to be on-camera . . . to have this kind of a fuss made over them.

"Isn't this why you got into the business?" he asked.

"Actually . . . no."

"Turn this way and fold your arms," he said.

"Please, no folded arms. Why are all the promo pictures of female anchors like this?" I demonstrated the classic pose. "I'm confused. What is this supposed to convey?"

Ellen sounded off behind me. "Hey, Jordan, the quicker you give him the shot, the sooner we can have drinks."

"Ooohh, Ellen. That was the motivation I was looking for."

I had been warned that these shoots could go on forever—a lot of hurry up and wait. I just didn't realize standing in place could be so exhausting. We wrapped just short of six hours, which didn't include the two extra hours for hair and makeup. The energy of finally being outside brought new life to us both. I coveted Ellen's more practical choice of footwear, a pair of brown suede boots she scored at DSW. She loved reminding me how much money I wasted buying shoes at full price. But "never pay full price" was my middle name. It also was my little secret that I conveniently withheld.

"What time is it?" I asked Ellen, one of the few people I knew who still wore a wristwatch. Her affinity for nostalgia, I surmised long ago, was part of what made her so good at her job. The integrity required to lead newsrooms was not talked about nearly enough at the journalism conferences I'd attended over the years. Instead, panelists espoused the power of the anchorman, but the men who hired those men—and they are always men—don't get called out often enough or in the way they should. I've watched some of them lurk around the newsroom slapping their top-dog evening anchor on the back as they all wink and nod and peer salaciously at just about every woman in the room. I've heard stories of news directors rating on-air women and even interns like a bunch of frat boys. These same men then pretend to be outraged when an executive gets called out as a serial sexual predator and becomes front-page news. They are as much to blame for the huge pay gap between women and men in the business as the general managers are. And don't get me started on the stories they deem newsworthy. A white guy in his fifties making seven figures may not be as likely to have his finger on the pulse of what is relevant. Ellen was a rare breed. No matter how successful she can and no doubt will become, fairness was her fuel and true, honest reporting, her north star.

"It's five-forty. Still want that drink?" she asked.

"Absolutely! There's a cute little wine bar on Randolph. It was in the entertainment kicker on our morning show today. It's just a couple blocks up," I said.

Feet sore from traipsing around in stilettos, I navigated along the uneven cracked concrete and loose debris booby-trapping the sidewalks. I didn't recognize my own neighborhood at this time of day. Newly minted techies who had recently descended on the area jostled past me. They were easy to spot in their graphic hoodies and tees and designer sneakers, rushing from workplaces with fully stocked refrigerators of hydrating soft drinks, never to experience the frustration of digging for loose change to purchase underwhelming snacks from a vending machine. By the time we arrived, the once-obscure little wine bar was already packed with them, proving once again that there was no more efficient free advertising than a worthy mention on a television news morning show.

"Looks like we made it just in time for happy hour," Ellen said.

"Shh, don't say that too loudly," I said. "I thought happy hour could get you arrested."

One of the most shocking things I learned about Illinois when I first moved here was the crazy ban on "happy hour." Though drunken driving deaths were a valid concern, the legislation banning the after-work pastime seemed like a ghost of Chicago's Prohibition past. In Austin, Texas, where I grew up, "happy hour" was practically government sanctioned.

I scanned the tiny bar for a comfy, cozy seat. A velvet couch in the back was already taken.

"Look!" Ellen pointed. "There are two seats at the end of the bar. Let's grab 'em."

We had barely sat down when an older gentleman walked over and placed two cocktail napkins in front of us. He looked a tad out of place in a hip new millennial hot spot. He reminded me of a bartender at one of Chicago's old-school steakhouses.

"He-e-y-y, Jordan Manning! Nice to see you, young lady. Welcome to Doc's!"

"Hello there. Why, thank you!"

I'll never get used to people actually recognizing me because they have watched my work. It's a head trip.

"What's your name?" I asked.

"I'm Sam. Pleased to meet you," he said, offering his hand.

"Nice to meet you, Sam."

"What would you like?"

"I'll have the espresso martini and she'll have . . ."

". . . a Chardonnay," Ellen said, "though not your best Chardonnay. Something in the mid-price range for me is fine."

"Okay, ladies. Coming up."

I swung the barstool around to face Ellen and tried to create our own little VIP section. We had a lot to talk about and I didn't want anyone eavesdropping on us.

"Still saving up for that trip to Ireland?" I asked.

"Yeah, this fall. I finally earned enough vacation to go for nine days without using all my time off for the year," she said.

"That's exciting!"

"I know. I can't wait. So what about you? Any trips coming up?"

"Uh, yeah, actually. My best friend's getting married in Saugatuck in May."

"You're the maid of honor?" Ellen asked.

"Yes, which means I have responsibilities."

"Then, my dear, that's not a vacation. That's work."

Lisette wanted what she wanted. Her vision for the perfect wedding was so specific that she barely let anyone lift a finger to help, including me.

"No, I don't really see it that way. I'm looking forward to it. It'll be interesting to see two families and groups of friends coming together. Her fiancé is white; he grew up in California. And I mean he personifies beach-boy culture. Blond, blue eyes, swimmer's build."

"He sounds dreamy," Ellen said. "How'd they meet?"

"They met in Saugatuck, actually. Lisette and I went there for the weekend and stayed at a rental on the beach. Mike, that's his name, and a friend of his from Italy, in fact, were visiting that weekend, too. Their connection was instant, you know. They don't live in the same city but somehow kept things going, even while he was working outside of the country for a few months."

"And they say long-distance relationships never work," Ellen said.

"Well, if you really love someone, a few thousand miles shouldn't be the thing that gets in the way of your happiness."

Dating long distance was always exciting in the beginning. Cards, letters, gifts and flowers, and hours spent talking on the phone. After a while, it simply wasn't enough and ended with the sad realization that one or neither of you were willing to make the sacrifices necessary to be together. Lisette and Mike were outliers, but there was a part of me that felt that maybe this was all happening a little too fast.

"So what was up with Mike's friend? Was he cute? Did you two stay in touch?" Ellen asked.

"Adorable. But like you said, most long-distance relationships don't survive, so it wasn't worth pursuing. Besides, an international lover isn't on my wish list."

Sam returned and sat down two glasses with generous pours, smiling wryly. "Enjoy, ladies."

Ellen held up her glass. "Wow! A bowl of wine. Way to flirt, Sam. Must be nice to have fans. I need to go out with you more often."

"You think he's flirting with me? He's old enough to be my father," I said.

"And when has that ever stopped them," Ellen muttered.

"To Justice Jordan." Ellen held up her glass.

"To true love," I said.

"Salud." Ellen lightly tapped my glass. "So what are you working on these days?"

"You really know how to kill a vibe, don't you?"

"Sorry."

"No, it's okay. I've been getting a lot of calls on the hotline, but nothing is fleshed out yet. I'm still waiting for the big one."

One of the things I loved most about the investigative unit was the autonomy. I didn't have to check in as often with the brass until I had something worth reporting.

"Well, you just watch. This Justice Jordan promo is going to cement your reputation in Chicago," Ellen said, her head bobbing as if the physical gesture made her words even more true. "In this city, you're officially a part of broadcast history."

Ellen was still in hype mode. Her enthusiasm was endearing, but she didn't understand that from my point of view, the new promo would place an even bigger target on my back, in and out of the newsroom. The people who believed I was the pathway to a ratings boost were no longer in the minority.

"And officially responsible for boosting the ratings," I added.

"Hmm," said Ellen, shifting her head to the side, feigning deep thought. "That part is true." She giggled. "But look, you finally have a chance to have a life. To travel, to fall in love. Heck, to get a dog."

I laughed. "No thanks. Can you see me with a dog?"

Ellen's smile faded into a more serious expression, and I got the feeling some sisterly advice was forthcoming.

"What?"

"Jordan, you're a beautiful, vibrant young woman. Live like one."

2

Thursday, March 12

The yellow police tape bordering the crime scene forced morning commuters to navigate the normally busy but organized lineup of people who make the daily trek past the Civic Opera House of Chicago to one of the vast numbers of office towers, each stepping off the curb and onto traffic-choked Wacker Drive to avoid the scrum of reporters and police.

Diana Sorano: We go to Jordan Manning reporting from the Civic Opera House, the scene of a tragic shooting last night. Jordan, I understand a suspect is now in custody. What else can you tell us about the investigation?

Jordan: Diana, I'm here outside the Civic Opera House in downtown Chicago, where two people leaving last night's performance were confronted by a gunman and shot just a few steps from where I am standing. A couple of bystanders who saw what was happening bravely tackled the shooter. Police have identified him as thirty-eight-year-old Guillermo Morales of Brighton Park. According to investigators, Morales is the estranged husband of one of the victims, Marlena Morales. The second victim has been identified as Dr. Matt Shackelford, a forty-eight-year-old pulmonologist from Lincoln Park. Last evening, Marlena posted pictures of the two on her Facebook page just before the curtain call of a production of *The Marriage of Figaro*. Police say after the performance, Morales confronted the couple outside the theater. He is expected in court this afternoon for a bond hearing. Police are calling this premeditated murder.

Our live broadcast cut away to a prerecorded interview with a witness, a Columbia College student, his voice animated and his face visibly processing the images replaying in his mind.

"He pulled the gun from his backpack. I can't believe I saw it all," he said.

Jordan: Diana, sadly, the estranged couple leave behind two children, ages seven and nine. This is Jordan Manning reporting. Back to you.

• •

By the midmorning broadcast, local news stations had created graphics. Some of them were over the top, with loud breaking news music meant to jolt viewers at home into paying attention. "Murder at the Civic Opera." The opera house is a cultural bastion where its patrons—sophisticated seniors, you might say—never dreamed a murder could take place inches from where they were enjoying an evening out in the city. Now add that it was a suspected crime of passion, and this was guaranteed to ignite a media frenzy. In a bizarre turn, and with so much of the crime in Chicago yet again getting national attention, it was even more astounding that it wasn't gang or drug related.

And a high-profile victim like Dr. Matt Shackelford, who sat on several boards and was a member of the Chicago Yacht Club, raised the stakes even higher for media outlets to out-work the competition and be the first to report snackable bits about the victims' backstories. The crime had been solved, but the fact that the killer had tracked down his victims on social media—an indication of its growing popularity and people's willingness to share their lives publicly—was also a part of this story. I couldn't explain why, but it gave me a sense of foreboding.

The scene outside the Circuit Court of Cook County at 26th and California was more of a circus than usual. Guillermo Morales's arraignment drew not only members of the press but women's advocacy groups, survivors of domestic violence, and self-proclaimed social media experts. Their reasons for being there were clear. They were using this story to advance their agenda, make a name for themselves, or both. It was the kind of true crime drama that, I suspected, would one day play out on the big screen. In fact, a colleague told me he'd heard that Court TV planned to set up shop in Chicago to cover every aspect of the case, including the trial.

As the A1, I didn't have to cover something as mundane and procedural as an arraignment. It's anticipated the defendant will plead not guilty, which is just a formality that gives their lawyer the slightest bit of leverage to negotiate a sentence with the prosecutor. My motive for being there was simple. I wanted to see the killer. What could I learn from his expression? My mentor, forensic scientist Dr. Marvin Chan, shared an observation back in grad school that has always stuck with me. He said, "A killer can hide his crimes behind words and even in his body language, but not in his eyes. The eyes don't lie."

By the time I pulled up to the courthouse in a taxi, the line to get inside the building snaked all the way down the steps to the sidewalk. I skipped past the hustle and bustle and walked half a block to an alternative way inside that was rarely used by or accessible to reporters. On the way, I dialed Deputy Jeanetta Cole and hoped that this would be one of those times when having a relationship paid off.

Come on, Ms. Cole. Pick up!

"Hello, this is Jeanetta."

"Hi! Ms. Cole! It's Jordan Manning. How are you?"

"I'm doing well," she said in an ebullient tone. "Are you here?" she asked, cutting to the chase in our familiar exchange.

"Yes, I'm at the courthouse, but the line at the main entrance is insane today. I'll never make it to my hearing. Can you do me a favor?"

"Sure. Come on now. You know where I am."

"Thank you! Thank you! I'm literally walking up right now."

I waved through the tiny window of the heavy steel door. Deputy Cole, who was sitting at the security desk, held up a finger and gestured to a colleague to take her place. She walked toward me, unlatching a ring of keys from her waist belt. The door made a terrible screeching sound and tripped an alarm that she quickly silenced with a press of a button.

"Hey, Jordan! Long time no see," she said. "Where've you been?"

Deputy Cole, the gatekeeper over this little fiefdom, was a thirty-year veteran of the force. And during that time, she had become a grandmother and earned a reputation as someone not to be played with. She was no rule breaker, though. She had her favorites; I just happened to be one of them. If I hadn't seen her featured on a local news segment, I might never have known she existed in this obscure corner of Cook County's judicial system. Still, she granted me a privilege I swore never to abuse and to treat with all due respect, which included fawning over pictures of her grandchildren taped to the glass barrier around the security desk for all to see. Nobody would dare move them.

"I thought you might be here today," she said. "Come on in."

"Thank you so much, Ms. Cole. You know I appreciate this. It's nuts out there," I said.

"This opera murder case. Whew! Tragic and senseless," she said.

"Yeah, I know," I said, "and the whole social media thing . . ."

"That's why I'm happy to be my age. I keep my business in my little black book. I don't go on Facebook. And I tell my kids to keep me off of there, too!"

There were only a few people ahead of me in the security line. Like everybody else, I did the dance of removing my coat and the contents of my pockets and placed my purse on the belt to be scanned.

"You better hurry. I heard them talking over the radio. They haven't opened the doors yet, but folks are about to be let in any minute now."

"Okay, I will! Thanks!"

I tried to call the newsroom to check in, but the call failed. The courthouse was notorious for having bad cell phone reception, and cell phones weren't allowed to be visible in the courtrooms, which is why reporters covering trials were seen frequently darting in and out to phone in updates. In the meantime, from the lower level, I had to face three flights of stairs to get to the second floor. I arrived just as deputies were allowing people to enter Judge Joan Simpkins's courtroom. I saw several familiar faces. The head of the opera, a women's rights advocate

I interviewed once, and folks who looked like the victims' family members I'd seen on the news. I grabbed a seat directly behind the prosecutor's table. It would provide easy access to the state's attorneys if I had questions and an unobstructed view of the defense table so I could get a good look at the defendant.

"All rise!" a deputy announced.

An expressionless Judge Simpkins emerged from her chambers. The most violent high-profile cases tended to land on her docket. It was almost a certainty that she would drop the hammer and deny bail in this one.

"Please be seated. These proceedings will now come to order. Call the first case," the judge ordered.

"The people versus Guillermo Morales!" the deputy shouted.

Flanked by two Cook County sheriff's deputies, Morales, shackled at the wrists and ankles, wearing an orange top and matching pants, shuffled in and over to the defense table. His head was bowed low, his chin resting on his chest. I couldn't see his eyes.

"The defendant will remain standing. Is the state prepared to read formal charges?" Simpkins asked.

"We are, Your Honor," said the state's attorney. "On the evening of March 11, 2009, the defendant, Guillermo Morales, thirty-eight years of age, of Brighton Park, used an online social media site to track the whereabouts of his estranged spouse, Marlena Morales, and her friend, Dr. Matthew Shackelford, with the intent to kill or commit bodily harm. Mr. Morales fired a handgun at the victims as they were exiting 20 North Upper Wacker Drive, striking each twice in the upper torso, causing their deaths. Police recovered a handgun registered to Mr. Morales at the scene. The state charges Guillermo Morales with two counts of murder in the first degree; stalking, a Class 4 felony;

and unlawful discharge of a firearm. Due to the premeditated nature of this crime, we ask that the defendant be remanded to custody without bond, Your Honor."

"Thank you, Mr. Cudahy."

The judge continued, "Defense, how do you answer?"

"Your Honor, may the record reflect that Mr. Morales is being represented by the Cook County public defender's office at these proceedings," said the court-appointed attorney, Delilah Turner.

"Duly noted. Mr. Morales, do you give your consent to be represented by the public defender?" the judge asked.

Morales stood silent, swaying slightly back and forth.

"Mr. Morales," prodded Simpkins. "Do you give your consent to be represented by this public defender?"

Speechless, Morales shook his head from side to side.

"Mr. Morales, I need verbal confirmation," Simpkins pressed on.

"No," he muttered.

"No?"

"No," he repeated.

"Your Honor, may I confer with my client?" the public defender asked.

"No!" Morales barked. "No!"

Whispers erupted in the courtroom, and the judge tapped her gavel to restore calm. "Mr. Morales, am I to understand that you have secured your own counsel?"

"Yeah. Me. I'm gonna be my own lawyer."

"Mr. Morales, I must warn you that if you act as your own attorney, this court will not be obligated to provide you with any legal advice or assistance to help you prepare your case. I'm talking zero assistance, do you understand?"

Morales again went on mute.

"Mr. Morales, do you understand what I'm telling you?"

"Yeah," he muttered.

"You understand that the charge of first-degree premeditated murder carries a mandatory sentence of life in prison? And that in addition to that charge, you face two additional felonies that carry sentences of between ten and thirty years? That if convicted, you would be facing life in prison without the possibility of parole?"

Morales nodded. "Mr. Morales, I need verbal confirmation that you understand what I'm telling you."

"Yes!" he bellowed.

"Your Honor, please, Mr. Morales is clearly under duress," Turner said. "I must insist on a moment to confer with my client."

"I am not your client!" Morales screamed. His body convulsed as his composure melted away.

"Mr. Morales, I have to agree with Ms. Turner that I believe you would benefit from some additional counsel before making this decision," Simpkins said.

"No-o-o-o!" Morales screamed and turned his body toward the spectators, his face twisted into a preternatural scornful sneer. His eyes burned with loathing.

Simpkins pounded the gavel. "Order!"

Morales, undeterred, continued his rant. "That whore took everything from me! My kids! My living! She killed me! She got what she deserved!"

"You bastard!" shouted a man from the back of the courtroom. "That was my sister! I'll kill you!"

"Order!" Simpkins pounded her gavel. "I'll have order or I'll clear this courtroom!"

Simpkins's call to order was no match for the screams and wails of family members and the gobsmacked gasps from on-lookers. But no one could have predicted what happened next. Morales lunged at the public defender and head-butted her with such force she fell backward, barely missing the sharp end of the prosecutor's table. As sheriff's deputies closed in on him, Morales banged his head against the defense table with such force that he slumped unconscious to the floor.

"Deputies, clear the courtroom! Now! Everybody out!" Simpkins ordered.

Oh my god. Is this really happening?

"Is she okay?" I said to no one in particular as the prosecutors and court reporter rushed to their unconscious colleague's side. Officers formed a barrier and moved everyone toward the exit. "Let's go! Let's go, people!"

I kept looking behind, hoping to see Delilah Turner up on her feet, shaken but conscious. She was out cold.

3

Thursday, March 12

Dusk painted the sky pink and yellow as Shelly Biltmore pulled her pickup truck onto the long gravel driveway leading up to the classic rustic farmhouse. It was a sizable place with an endless front yard that dwarfed the manicured lawns of the mansions of Highland Park Estates, a star-studded neighborhood on the dreamy North Shore of Illinois. Now, with Marla and both of their parents gone, it was too much house for one person, with four bedrooms unused day in and day out. But Shelly was still drawn to it, because some of the best times of her life had been spent in that house. The walls held memories, far too many to count, but all leading to a feeling of a life that was. There were times she would wake up and her half-awakened mind would believe the smell of her mother's vanilla pancakes was real. The hardest, though, were the dinners alone at the dining room table, the empty chairs once occupied with people long gone or in the case of Marla, rarely seen.

Shelly headed upstairs, walking past the closed bedroom doors to the lone one now occupied. Peeling off her work clothes to change into sweatpants was the "rinse, repeat" action that ended every day. No sooner had she plopped down into a well-worn recliner than the phone rang.

"Hello?"

"Auntie Shell!"

Shelly's heart pounded. Her nephew sounded panicked, and now so was she. Had he read the newspaper articles? Seen the TV coverage? Surely his father and grandparents were doing everything they could to shield Cameron from any speculative reports about his mother's whereabouts, or whether she had been harmed.

"Cammy! My sweet boy, how are you doing?"

At age eight, Cameron Hancock was just mature enough to try and mask his feelings. "Okay," he said, drawing out the word, his voice revealing worry. "When's Mom coming home?"

It was a question that broke Shelly's heart into tiny pieces. Should she pretend everything was okay? Or did she tell this child of only eight years the truth outright? *No one knows where your mother is, or when or whether she'll ever come back.*

It had been nearly three weeks since Marla was a no-show to pick up her kids from school. Calls to her cell phone that day went straight to voicemail, which happened only when her phone was turned off or her battery was dead. And both possibilities were unlikely on a school day. Marla was obsessed with preventing her cell phone from running out of juice. She wouldn't leave the house until it was fully charged. Her car had also vanished, and she left all her belongings behind, the most stunning omission being her two children, the younger, Dara, just four years old.

Marla's husband, Jim, showed up in Rensselaer, Indiana, from Danville, Kentucky, a six-hour drive, the very next morning to retrieve his children. He got there so fast Shelly wondered if he had been in town all along. He hadn't seen the kids since his and Marla's estrangement began four months earlier. Shelly didn't even have a chance to say goodbye to her beloved niece and nephew. She was busy rounding up friends to form a search party and being interviewed by police and a reporter at the *Rensselaer Republican* newspaper. Volunteers were out scouring every corner of the bedroom community. Even the sorghum fields on the Biltmore farm six miles outside of town were being swept as Jim swooped into town, grabbed the kids, and skipped.

"Shelly, Jim had every right to come get his kids," Victoria, Marla's best friend from high school, told Shelly over the phone. "I know you don't like him, but . . ."

"I never said he didn't, Victoria," Shelly shot back defensively. "I just wish I would've known. Don't you realize, I may never see them again?"

Marla was struggling to make it on her own. She was broke, unemployed, and in the middle of a custody battle when she moved back to their hometown of Rensselaer.

"Take your time. There's no rush. I'm here for you," Shelly had told her.

Having Marla and the kids back home was the happiest Shelly had been in a while. Sitting on the back porch of their family's eighty-year-old farmhouse, the sisters savored sips of bourbon one night and talked under a starry sky. Shelly encouraged Marla to take some time for herself before coming up with a game plan.

"You just got here," Shelly told her. "You're okay now. There's nothing you and those kids need that cannot be provided for here."

"What if he comes here? What if I can't get a job? I'm scared," Marla had said.

"You're home, Marl. You've got people here who have your back just like he does in Danville where he grew up. Nothing's gonna happen to you. You're safe. Take all the time you need."

Even people who say things like "Take your time" have their limits. Shelly hadn't nearly reached hers. Marla got there first. Their almost daily fights over what Shelly saw as Jim's manipulation of her sister and Marla's constant bending to his will eroded Shelly's influence. Marla's coy and accommodating demeanor became increasingly obstinate and mercurial. Then one day she was gone.

"I don't know yet, bud," Shelly told her nephew. "But I'll tell you what I'm gonna do."

Cam expelled an exasperated sigh. Even a boy his age could detect the smoke and mirrors. "What?"

"I'm going to keep my cell phone on me all the time, even when I'm asleep, so I won't miss her call," she said convincingly, though she was losing faith that the call would ever come.

"And you'll let me know, right?" the boy implored.

"Roger that, Green Ranger. I promise."

Shelly pressed her ear to the receiver and listened for the smile she used to be able to detect just by the way he was breathing. Their bond was especially tight. Marla, who was three years younger than Shelly, admired but also envied their connection. Shelly and her nephew were kindred spirits. He shared her vibrant hair color, and both were subjected to every stereotype of a ginger one could think of. Yet both were the most sensitive people in every room. When he was taunted by the other cousins and friends one holiday, it was Shelly who swooped in, growling "Back off!" when the taunts went too far.

Shelly convinced Cam that his red hair was a superpower, a secret weapon. Shelly and Cam found many ways to satisfy their imaginary musings. Lately, their playful interactions had been inspired by the *Power Rangers* TV series. They each took on the persona of their favorite character. Shelly leaned into that familiarity now, praying it would help her convey what she dared not speak plainly. *Spy on your dad for me.*

"Oh, one more thing, Green Ranger . . ." Shelly said in a masculine voice.

"Yes, Pink Ranger," Cam responded, lowering his octave to match his aunt's.

"Remember, we're on a secret mission. I'm counting on you. Seek truth and report back anything unusual. You've got your weapon?"

"The Nikon?"

"That's the one, Green Ranger. Take pictures. Let's power up!"

"Roger, Blue Ranger!" he said, his mood brightening. "May the power protect you!"

"And you," she said.

Cameron had gotten pretty good with the throwaway cameras. But after witnessing a huge blowout between Marla and her husband, Shelly lent the boy her digital. The video and easy upload capabilities of a digital camera were the closest she would come these days to having a clue about what was going on in that house.

In the weeks since Marla vanished, the volunteers eventually abandoned the search and police still didn't have any leads. They were able to track pings off Marla's phone from the nearest cell phone tower, which indicated she was no longer in Indiana. But eventually the pings stopped. Her battery must have died. Shelly knew that if Marla was somewhere safe and alive, she would never have let that happen. But until her worst fear could be confirmed, Shelly busied herself with running the farm while also moonlighting at a horse stable in Greenwood two hours away on the weekends. The crying fits and overall stress of these tumultuous days had begun to take a toll on her physically. She felt a constant stabbing in her chest as if she'd been kicked by one of the Arabian horses she groomed. She knew the pressure buildup would eventually burst, but she never dreamed anything like this could happen, not while her eyes were open.

Updates from the sheriff's department had been nonexistent the past few days. So after she hung up with Cam, Shelly called Jasper County's lead investigator, Lieutenant Bob Flanagan, but the switchboard operator picked up.

"How may I direct your call?" said the operator.

"Put me through to Flanagan, please," Shelly said.

"May I ask who's calling?"

"This is Shelly Biltmore trying to get an update on my sister's case."

"One moment," the operator said.

Shelly had left three messages in as many days and wasn't hopeful she would get through this time, either. It seemed to Shelly that the police were giving up. While on hold, she muttered to herself, "If this SOB makes me leave another message, I—"

"Miss Biltmore," said the lieutenant, startling her. "How may I help you?"

"You know why I'm calling, Lieutenant Flanagan. Where are you with this investigation?"

"Miss Biltmore," he said, "I assure you I will inform you of any progress or updates. Our investigation is ongoing. That's all I can tell you right now."

"Did you alert the Danville police? Have they spoken with her husband?" Shelly pressed on.

"Miss Biltmore, Marla's husband has an airtight alibi.

There's nothing that would lead investigators to believe that he had anything to do with your sister's absence."

"You mean my sister's *disappearance*," Shelly corrected him.

"Miss Biltmore . . ."

"Sir! I am very well aware of my name!" she spouted off. "Thanks for nothing!"

Shelly slammed down the retro receiver of the old black telephone that had occupied the living room since she was a girl. "Damn it! What can I do?" she said to no one.

Shelly paced the floor. Tears streaked her face. Her thoughts turned dark as her anger and frustration with the stonewalling by the sheriff's department made her seriously contemplate putting her fist through a wall. She opted for a distraction instead, and turned on the television, curling up in the overstuffed recliner. The tears didn't stop, igniting the natural melatonin in her brain. Before long, she fell into a deep sleep, awakened a couple of hours later by the alert of an email notification coming from her laptop. It was now fully dark out. The TV had been watching her nap. She awoke just as the blaring music of the evening news echoed through her quiet living room. Shelly's eyes adjusted to the light from the television before the headline came into focus: "Murder at Chicago's Civic Opera House" just to the right of the new anchor's head in a square with the exterior of the opera house above the words.

Anchor: Tonight, we're following up on the murders outside Chicago's Civic Opera House and the suspect's bizarre courtroom attack a day after being arrested for gunning down his estranged wife and her friend. Thirty-eight-year-old Guillermo Morales violently assaulted his public defender today at his bond hearing. In Chicago, for more on this story, correspondent Jordan Manning.

Jordan: Guillermo Morales's bond hearing started with a combative exchange with Judge Joan Simpkins. The suspect in the deadly attack at the civic opera screamed "No!" when asked if he accepted public defender Delilah Turner as counsel. Then his erratic behavior turned violent.

The video cut to an interview with state's attorney Mark Cudahy. "This guy was agitated from the moment he walked into the courtroom. He was screaming at the judge. Everybody was looking at him, but there was nothing we could do. He turned and slammed his head into hers. It was like it was happening in slow motion. When I think of how close she came to hitting that desk. He could've killed her."

Shelly sat up in her chair.

Jordan: Morales then proceeded to slam his head against the defense table, knocking himself unconscious and suffering a concussion. He has additionally been charged with second-degree assault and was denied bond. Public Defender Delilah Turner's injuries are not life threatening. She is still under observation at Rush University Medical Center. But as the state's attorney alluded, this could have been a lot worse.

How horrible.

Shelly grabbed her laptop and typed "opera Chicago shooting" into the Google search engine. She clicked on an AP story. As she read the words *estranged husband* and *murdered*, her heart pounded. *What is it with these men who can't just leave? They have to kill? And he found her by tracking her on her Facebook post!*

Shelly's cell phone rang.

"Hello, Cam? Hey, what's going on, bud? Are you okay?" she asked, shielding the panic and concern over the fact that her nephew had called her back that very evening.

"Pink Ranger," he said, projecting his little kid's voice in such a way that was almost comical. "Power up! Check your email. I gotta go."

"Okay, bud. I mean, Green Ranger."

Shelly grabbed her laptop and clicked on an image of a screenshot.

That's Jim's screen name. That bastard! Who's he talking to?

Shelly clicked back over to the Google search of the news story and found a link to the Channel 8 News segment. She watched it until the end but didn't learn anything more than what she'd seen on her television moments ago. She hit the back button and arrived on the Channel 8 News home page and scrolled to the bottom. A video began to play automatically.

"No matter where the story leads her, Justice Jordan is on the case."

Shelly recognized the reporter as the one who covered the murder at the opera. She searched "Jordan Manning" on the news site and came upon a headline from a few months ago: "Channel 8 Crime Reporter Helps Police Catch a Serial Killer."

4

Monday, March 16

Geesh. What time is it? It took me a moment to recognize the disorienting vibrating sound in my bedroom. Half-awake, I glanced at the clock on my dresser, but a wine glass sediment-stained red, evidence of my routine way of de-stressing at night, blocked my view.

A week into daylight saving time, it was still dark outside, but the draft from the partly open window next to my bed made it feel more like midwinter. The blinds were pulled down to just above the windowsill, so dim light from the high-rise buildings filtered in, but not enough to help me locate what I now realized was my cell phone ringing.

You've got to be kidding—6:03 A.M.! Why-y-y-y?

I grabbed the phone just as the vibrating stopped and clicked on a message from Jenny B. The words on the screen generated a riptide of anxiety. **Breaking news.** For the viewer, those words can set off the "What bad news now?" alarm. But to a journalist, they stand for "It's go time." I'd lain awake many nights with the breaking news theme music playing over and over in my head like an earworm I couldn't shake, even in my dreams.

So what was it this time? A homicide? An arrest? Had an arson fire torn through an apartment building packed with families? This wasn't macabre; it was my reality. And at times it made me wonder why I ever decided to do this job.

I sat up too quickly and my body pleaded, "Go back to sleep," threatening, "If you try to stand up, I will drop you to the floor."

HEY JORDAN. R U UP? - J.B.

A better question would be "Jordan, do you ever sleep?" More often than I care to admit, I've wondered whether I could ever have a husband or a child with this schedule. *Mommy's got to go. There was a huge explosion in Kankakee, a suspected arson. They say it's one of the worst ever in the state. Every station is sending crews ASAP.* Would they understand?

In truth, the bona fide version of my new A1 status was far more mundane than I realized it would be. There were days when I missed standing shoulder to shoulder with other news crews, crammed in front of a sea of mic stands waiting for a police update or hoping to lob the question that made the evening news. Monday through Friday, in the Channel 8 newsroom by noon, reporting a live shot at six and then the lead spot for the main broadcast at ten. At least with weekends off, I thought I'd have more time to date and finally take that girls' trip I'd been talking about for months. But instead I spent most weekends scanning newspapers and magazines, looking for stories to pitch in the Monday news meeting, where producers and editors vie for the day's lead story. I spent hours listening to voicemails left for me at work and pored over incoming emails with tips.

"Jordan, what do you want to be? A reporter or a detective?" The chorus of people questioning my obsession to find the next big story was getting louder, and so were my doubts about a future in broadcast journalism. I was stuck on "Why can't I be a reporter who actually investigates versus waiting for the police to tell me what to put in my report?" This was precisely the reason why, for so long, reporters have described suspects as "Black male, five-eleven, wearing a blue shirt." A million people could fit that generic description. But police frequently offer very little detail, and reporters simply regurgitate what police say without thinking about the consequences. That can set off a dangerous situation that results in racial profiling, and even worse, a deadly confrontation between police and an innocent person.

I needed a "deep breath in, sigh it out" moment before replying to Jenny B. I'M UP. WHAT'S GOING ON? Before launching into work mode, I wanted to at least wash my face. I remembered the sample of a lush face wash I'd left by the sink. A salesperson handed it to me the other day as I walked through the cosmetics section at Bloomingdale's on North Michigan Avenue. The tiny bottle, not even two ounces, would have been a splurge for me. People mistakenly believed that everyone on television earned millions, especially in Chicago, where some lead local anchors landed multimillion-dollar, multi-year contracts. I had been promoted, but did it come with a raise? No.

The struggle to open the annoying sample-sized container was worth it once the foam emulsified into every pore in my face. *Note to self: Go back for another handful of samples.*

No matter how good it felt, it wasn't enough to distract me from the "breaking news" message that I had yet to deal with. And there was no better bearer of bad news than Jenny Bernardi, the overnight desk assistant, or Jenny B., as she was known around the station to distinguish her from Jenny Agovino, who worked afternoons. Jenny B. answered the newsroom hotline between one A.M. and nine A.M. To her fell the arduous task of listening to people's desperate, panicked pleas for help. But it also made her privy to some of the biggest stories as they were developing. So I invited her to call me no matter the time. Why not? We were both single, no kids, and the last time I checked, neither of us had any prospects who would "put a ring on it." Work was our life.

I GOT A WEIRD EMAIL OF A SCREENSHOT WITH A NOTE SAYING "I NEED JORDAN MANNING TO SEE THIS."

Don't hurt yourself on the details, Jenny, I wrote back.

CHECK YOUR EMAIL.

Hang on. Let me get to my computer.

I walked over to a compact desk I had bought at Target and proudly assembled on my own. Tucked into the corner of my bedroom, it served as my home office. I had been warned by my physician pal Courtney Blackwell never to put an office in the bedroom, because as she said, "It disrupts the tranquility where you sleep. Boundaries!" But my apartment is small, so where else was I going to put it? I signed into my account and opened the email marked Urgent that Jenny B. had forwarded to me. I downloaded and opened an attachment. It was a picture of a computer screen and what appeared to be a screenshot of a conversation two people were having online.

rubble&rock: She's not even a good mom.

Hapinfast: Well, isn't that the point of the divorce. To finally get rid of her?

rubble&rock: Only one way to be sure.

Hapinfast: What do you have in mind?

rubble&rock: I thought you wanted to play for keeps.

This is why you woke me up?

The newsroom hotline had been lighting up with two dozen or more callers a day pleading for my help ever since the Justice Jordan promo started running. The spots were even on the radio. "Justice Jordan. Fighting for you. Only on Channel 8." It was in such heavy rotation, I was overwhelmed.

"Can I speak to Jordan Manning?" "Can Jordan Manning call me back?" "I don't want to speak to anybody but Jordan." "Help me. Please." I told Jenny B.: "Feel free to reach out to me if a hotline call meets two criteria: One, time is of the essence, and two, it sounds legit. Anytime."

If there was anything urgent about this weird back-and-forth, it certainly was lost on me. If anything, it sounded like a bad breakup. I sympathized with Jenny B. for having to listen to countless sob stories and prank calls, being yelled at and called names. Her frustration was valid. Anyone would end up jaded if exposed to this day in and day out. But Jenny B. lacked empathy, and I found her dismissive tone and the way she mocked and made fun of people who were in distress appalling. While oftentimes they were complaining in vain, many of the people calling in, from their perspective, did believe they had been wronged.

In spite of my skepticism about the urgency, I called her.

"News Channel 8."

"Hey, Jenny, it's Jordan. Come *o-o-on*," I said, yawning loudly. "You've GOT to give me more than that."

"This lady said her sister's missing, and she thinks her husband did something to her," she said.

I was processing what she was telling me when . . . "Jordan!" she snapped. "Are you there?"

I wasn't all there. At least not yet. I hadn't even had my first sip of coffee.

"Jordan, did you hear me?" she persisted.

You woke me at the crack of dawn. Give me a chance to clear my head.

"A woman missing? Her husband might be involved? That's horrible. Did she leave a number?" I asked.

"Not sure. I sent her to your voicemail."

"Okay. Jenny, you are my official alarm clock. Look, let me get myself together. My first meeting isn't until noon, but I'll come in early. You'll be gone soon, though, right?"

"No, I'll still be here. I'm covering the desk for part of the next shift," she said.

"Okay, I'll see you in an hour."

Technically, I didn't have to be at work for another six hours to make the noon planning meeting, which was the handoff to the evening news. I'd been a regular at the meetings since gaining some notoriety for helping police catch a serial killer. It should have made me feel accomplished but instead left me conflicted over being a so-called vigilante. At what price? I sometimes struggled to see my success as the by-product of heartbreak and death. And for sure, I never intended for my role on the crime unit to take the form of the Jordan Manning Detective Agency.

I dialed into my work phone to hear the message Jenny B. was certain the caller had left for me. She was right; there was a message. I found myself pressing the phone so tightly to my ear that the pressure vibrated in my head. The more firmly I pressed, the more muffled the faint voice became. I couldn't make out a single word of what was said. Just muffled whispers that dissolved into white noise. Even more frustrated now, I replayed the voice message but got the same result.

What is this? A joke?

I laid back down and stared at the ceiling. My sluggishness was the direct result of the now empty bottle of pinot noir sitting on the kitchen counter. It served its purpose—temporarily numbing my heart. Today was his birthday. The Pisces gallant who lived rent free in my head was back for a stay. For how long this time? Lin was my first love and first lover. He would always occupy a special place in my heart. But I didn't owe him my peace of mind. I broke up with him eight years ago. Eight years! I'd replayed that ugly scene over and over and wished I could edit it out and voice it over like an embarrassing mistake in a taped interview. I had expected him to feel hurt, but he was furious with me. *Please, God, give me the strength to mute this memory. Let me live without this constant reminder that I had my shot at love and blew it.*

"Jordan, you compare every guy you meet to Lin, and that's not fair to the next guy," Mom said after I ended it with a handsome pilot I was introduced to a couple years back.

Lin wasn't to blame. He had done everything he could to be the man he thought I wanted or needed him to be. Ultimately,

I decided there was no way for him to be what I wanted, because I had no idea what I even wanted. I was twenty-two years
old and figured there would be plenty of time and options in
the future. I followed the prevailing wisdom that marrying so
young would be the same as throwing my life away. Now, at
thirty, I could hear the unmistakable creak of a door slowly
closing on milestones I had set aside for my career.

"That's your biological clock ticking," Courtney theorized.

"Nah!" I huffed. "That's not it."

Wasn't it? Courtney is an ob/gyn and mother of two married to a man who is also a doctor and living in a six-bedroom,
four-bath house in the suburbs with a three-car garage. She
managed to get all that and a career. She sacrificed nothing she
valued. Where did I get the notion that a career and falling in
love and having a family must be mutually exclusive? Somewhere along the way, this point of view became my truth. Now
Lisette was the latest to defy that logic and Lin Jackson once
again had my stomach in knots.

Did I mess up?

5

Entering the newsroom had become intense. When I first started in the business, a station would maybe have a security guard for hire set up in the lobby. Now, ever since an irate viewer had viciously attacked a guard, putting him in the hospital, there were two: one in a secure booth at the building's entrance and another parked just outside the newsroom. Whether it was someone angry over a story or obsessed with the on-air talent, going from hero to target of hate was part of what it meant to work in the media world now more than ever. When I was in college, being a war correspondent was considered a dangerous reporting gig. Now even local news reporters had to watch their back as the "blame the media" crowd was getting bolder.

Just as I was about to swipe my security badge to go inside, I got a call from Lisette Holmes, one of my closest friends. Last night the soon-to-be Mrs. Spencer was in full bridal melt-down. We were on the phone until one-thirty in the morning. I recalled little of our conversation, only that her voice turned shrill as she filled me in on every detail of the caterer from hell, whom she insisted was about to ruin the most beautiful wedding to take place on the shores of Saugatuck, a charming beach town in Michigan. I started to nod off at some point between "They're messing with the wrong one" and the more dignified written response she finally settled on. "Okay, how about 'This is unacceptable, but I know you'll get it right. I very much look forward to your correcting these mistakes'?"

If there was an Oscar for code switching, Lisette would have won one by now. She better than anyone understood how the "scary Black woman" label could be slapped on our foreheads. So watch your tone and reread the email before hitting send.

"What kind of maid of honor falls asleep on the bride over the phone?"

Uh-oh. I smiled to myself.

"Good morning!" I said.

"Mm-hmm," she said.

"What time did we get off the phone last night? Did I fall asleep?"

"You know you did," said Lisette, never missing a moment to call me out. "How much did you hear?"

"I don't know. What'd I miss?"

When I was barely ten feet inside the newsroom, before Lisette could answer, Jenny B. shouted my name louder and raspier than necessary, especially at this time of morning, when the newsroom was fairly empty and quiet.

"Girl, who is yelling your name?" Liz asked. "It's eight o'clock. Are you at work already?"

"Yeah, I came in early. Remember that woman I told you about on the overnight desk?" My answer again was interrupted by Jenny B.'s fire-engine screech of a voice.

"There's a hotline for you," Jenny B. said, clearly now even more annoyed because she could see my cell phone pressed against my ear. Whatever call I was on couldn't be more important than her need to get my attention. "It's some guy. He sounds drunk. You want it?"

"Liz, I'm gonna have to call you back."

"Okay," Liz said. "Call me later."

The involuntary eye roll was so intense that even if Jenny B. didn't see it, I know she felt it. This was my life. My new normal. Not enough sleep, in the newsroom hours before my shift and sometimes long past it to prepare for the next day. Repeat. Except it was no longer new, just overwhelming. Putting on the armor I wore at Channel 8 outside the comfort zone of friends and family was how I coped with it.

"Good morning, Jenny. Did you say he sounded drunk?" I said in the most disarming way possible, a lot less southern than I was a few seconds ago with Lisette, but not what somebody like Jenny B. would consider hostile. Just as Jenny was about to speak, I interjected, "Hold on. I'll be right back."

"Just wait a minute . . ." she began before I turned back to her and said, "I promise."

She gaped at me, the words left unsaid, but her eyes showed she was clearly offended that I had cut her off. It was amazing how many people in this building believed they were my boss. That now included the overnight desk assistant, who wasn't even a manager but felt she had the authority to admonish me nonetheless. It made me think back on something that the sole Black female professor I had as an undergraduate told me. She said, "When it comes to Black women working in offices, everybody seems to believe they're our boss. Yet too often you will be seen as the bossy one." Most women relate to this dynamic in some way. But the extra burden is something women of color on every level, even in executive offices, push down to some deep compartment hidden from the world not to be shared, except on rare occasions over tears and wine.

Scripted scenes of reporters getting high fives in the newsroom and celebrating a big story with their colleagues were just that—scripted and seen only in the movies. At the end of the day, this was a competitive and cutthroat business.

I headed to the break room and caught a whiff of the overnight editor's fresh brew as he walked toward the edit bay to screen footage taken from car crashes, fires, and the aftermath of a fight that turned deadly outside a nightclub. I popped in a K-Cup and grabbed as many packages of cream and sugar as my hand could hold and headed for my desk. I caught Jenny B. out of the corner of my eye. Clearly, a caller was on hold. It was impossible to miss. She pointed the receiver at me, gesturing like an orchestra conductor.

"Got a call for you. You wanna take it?" she said.

"Who is it? It's not the drunk guy, is it?"

"No, it's the woman I told you about this morning," Jenny B. said. "She's called a billion times, Jordan."

"After listening to her voicemail earlier, I don't know what to make of her story. I couldn't even hear anything. Can you get her information and tell her I'll call her back? I just walked in."

"Okay! I'll tell her to leave you another voice message," Jenny said, giving me an incredulous stare.

"Wait." I sighed. "Go ahead and patch her through."

As I walked to my desk, I made a mental note that one day I would have to deal with Jenny B.

"Okay, sending her over to you now."

I grabbed my planner and answered on the first ring while I searched for a clean page to jot down notes. "Jordan Manning."

Silence.

"Hello, are you there? It's Jordan Manning. How can I help you?"

"Jordan? Finally! Is it really you?"

"Yes, this is Jordan."

A call waiting tone interrupted our connection.

"Wait, wait. I have to call you back. I am so sorry."

I heard a click and a dial tone. *She's gone? What is going on here? If she's so desperate, why'd she hang up?* I surmised from the voicemail that this was probably nothing. Just another weirdo.

Instead of yelling across the newsroom, as Jenny B. had earlier, I walked over to the desk. "She hung up," I said. "What the hell is going on with this woman?"

Jenny B. shrugged.

"Look," I said, dropping my voice an octave, "next time, get the number, please. I have no way of contacting her."

"I am sure she'll call back," she said, far more congenial than earlier. Perhaps it was my obvious change in tone, signaling I'd had just about enough. The balls of my feet provided the lift-off I needed to pivot and avoid snagging the heels of my stilettos on the carpet, and I walked away at a cadence I hoped Jenny B. read as "This conversation is over."

6

There was still an hour to go before the morning news meeting. I'd already killed time scanning the TV screens that lined the wall to the right of my desk, each tuned to a different news station. Some days, watching the competition just to make petty comments was a reporter's pastime. The scene could disintegrate into juvenile wisecracks in an instant. By now, all the local morning shows were over, and it was almost comical watching the muted screens flash random game shows, daytime talk shows, and hosts with catchphrases like "Let's talk about it" and the like. Filler until the noon newscast was how I saw it.

Scrolling through my cell phone . . . L, M, N . . . until I found Nate, which was how I listed him in my contacts after Nathan Fisher kept reminding me at dinner, "It's just Nate. My mother calls me Nathan."

"Well, okay," I had said, "Nate it is."

My best friend had fallen in love and was about to marry a man who most of her friends and family would have deemed the least likely of suitable matches for her. That is, until they saw the two of them together. Liz and Mike beamed in each other's presence. Their joy was palpable, and now their love story was chipping away at my cynicism about relationships. That's one way to explain why I decided to call Nate Fisher. Boredom and ego were others. At any rate, I had an excuse to get off the phone if the call went south. Who could argue with "breaking news"?

The phone had already rung twice by the time I regretted my decision to call. It was too late to hang up when the first-year medical resident at Northwestern answered.

"What's up?" he said.

I instantly regretted making the call. *What's up?* is something you say to one of your boys, not to a woman you're interested in.

"Hi, it's Jordan. Good morning. I'm good." Not that he'd asked. "How are you?"

"Good."

That's it? I'm going to need you to be a little more excited to hear from me. It sounded like he was in the car.

"Are you on your way to the hospital?"

"Yep."

What's with the one-word answers?

"Is everything okay?" I asked.

"Look, Jordan, I'm surprised to hear from you. Let's be real. That wasn't a good date."

It wasn't? It wasn't the best time I'd ever had, but it was decent enough for me to place this phone call. Why'd you kiss me, then, if it was so bad? Nate had gone from bold to blunt. I was caught off guard.

"What do you mean?"

"It was clear you weren't feeling me," he said.

He was partly right. The kiss was nice, but everything leading up to that moment felt rehearsed. But how did he know?

"Why do you say that?" I asked.

"Look, a man can tell, okay? Did you want something?" he asked.

Why did I call this man again?

By now my humiliation was complete. *How do I respond to that? I'd rather talk to Jenny B. right now.*

"Nate, the kiss was nice, but . . ."

"Were you calling to ask me out again?"

I didn't ask you out the first time! Was he joking? The people pleaser in me spoke first. "Yes. Sure, why not? I figured we could go out for drinks."

What have I done? Why didn't I just say goodbye? Was it because he was rejecting me?

"Cool. When?"

"How about Friday?"

"Great," he said. "Let's talk later this week to firm things up. Okay? I gotta go."

"Okay, but—"

He hung up before I could even say goodbye. It was clear to me then that second date was never going to happen. Why do people think it is easier to find a mate living in a big city? More choice? Ha! During my four years here, Chicago had yet to prove itself to be fertile ground, not for me anyway, so commitment had to take a back seat to fun. Unfortunately, Nate Fisher wasn't that much fun.

7

"Good morning, early riser!" Ellen waved and nodded toward me from a few feet away. I hadn't seen her enter the newsroom. By the time I looked in her direction, she'd walked in her office and popped right back out and walked hurriedly over to the news desk to talk to the assignment editor. From the moment Ellen walked into the office, she was always rushing and running.

I eased over to the news desk and listened in, sliding up next to Ellen with no shame. I wasn't being a nosy neighbor. On the news desk, all conversations are fair game. If you're not willing to snoop, you don't get the scoop. I overheard Ellen talking on the phone about a chemical fire burning out of control at a large industrial complex about an hour south of the city.

"They're evacuating residents. Now? Uh-huh. The fire marshal suspects arson. Okay, but if it's not safe, get out of there." Ellen hung up and glanced at me. "Hey, Jordan."

"Hey, what's going on?" I asked.

"Big fire at a plastics factory in Calumet City. The fumes are so bad they're telling folks to get out of there. Simone is on it."

When I moved up, my colleague Simone Michele was promoted from the overnight reporter to my old shift. Now she was doing live shots for the noon news.

"I didn't think this was one you'd want anyway," said Ellen, apologizing for something I hadn't accused her of doing. Our relationship had its ups and downs, but she walked a finer line than was necessary.

"You're right. I don't."

True, I was bored, but not bored enough to drive thirty miles to the Indiana state line for something that might make a juicy headline at noon but by ten P.M. would be nowhere near the lead story. Plus, there was no reason to think it would turn into an investigation.

"You're in early—again," Ellen said. "Why? What's up?"

"Jenny B. called me this morning. She said this woman had been blowing up the hotline asking for me. Says her sister is missing, and she thinks her husband might have hurt her. But when Jenny patched her to my phone, the woman hung up. She left a voicemail earlier with her number, but the connection was so bad I couldn't make it out."

"When's the last time she called?"

"Shortly after I got in, just after eight o'clock," I said.

"You've been here since eight!" Ellen said with a nervous laugh.

"Yes, but have I learned my lesson? No."

"She hasn't called back since?" Ellen asked. "Did you get where she's from?"

"No, nothing. Not even her name. Her voice was so low and muffled on the voicemail, it sounded like static. I couldn't make it out. Almost like she was whispering."

Ellen faded out, deep in thought.

"What?" I asked.

"I saw something on the wire recently about a missing mom. But it was out of Indiana, I think. Hold on. Let me see if I can find it again."

The screens on her desktop switched as she logged into

the LexisNexis online portal. It's a database of almost every story or every person, a research weapon that few viewers know exists. Ellen customized her account to get news alerts from the tri-state area, which consisted of northeastern Illinois, northwestern Indiana, and southeastern Wisconsin. As she scrolled through several pages, I tried to read each one that came and went within seconds. She stopped. "Wait . . . I think this is it. Yes, here it is. I was right. It's from a paper in Indianapolis."

Ellen clicked on the story link, and I rested against the back of her chair and leaned in.

"Mother of 2, Native Hoosier, Reported Missing," the headline read.

INDIANAPOLIS (AP)—The family of a 35-year-old mother of two from Danville, Kentucky, who had recently moved back to her native Rensselaer, Indiana, has reported her missing. Marla Hancock was last seen four days ago dropping off her 4-year-old daughter at a day care on East Angelica Street. Relatives say she was a no-show for two afternoon appointments: a job interview with a temp agency and a scheduled visit to see an apartment.

She was last seen driving a 2002 blue Toyota RAV4 with Kentucky license plate number AEO795.

This woman had recently moved back home with her family and was looking for a job and an apartment. It was easy to read between the lines.

"Sounds like she was trying to make a new start. The husband's got my vote for number one suspect."

"Maybe," Ellen said.

"That's what my mystery caller thinks, too. Wonder if there's a connection," I said.

"Check the date. This story is already several weeks old, and it doesn't mention any connection to her and Chicago or the suburbs," Ellen said.

"How far away is Rensselaer?" I was still learning the region's geography.

"A good hour and a half, and that's without traffic," she said. "It's too far."

Rensselaer was part of our meteorologist's regional forecast. *If it's too far, why does he provide weather updates there?*

"We cover McHenry County. It can take that long to get to some of those small towns up there," I said.

Local news markets were cash strapped, and coverage rarely extended beyond their boundaries because of budget limitations and viewer interest. Not to mention more people were gravitating to cable news. Heated fights and over-the-top personalities were the new stars of television. So before Ellen could answer and before I found myself in another back-and-forth with her over who and what we should be covering, I shut it down.

"It's probably not connected," I said, though I hadn't fully abandoned the idea that this story and the caller could be connected. I brought it up in the news meeting, with next to nothing to go on, but was loath to admit I had nothing else to offer.

"I got this cryptic hotline call about a missing mom. I'm following up," I said, hoping news director Peter Nussbaum would be satisfied and move on. But Peg Strahler, the metro editor, spoke up.

"Who's the victim? Where's she from?" she asked.

The only thing worse than not having anything to contribute during the meeting was giving a weak answer to a good question.

"The voicemail was hard to decipher. That's why I said it was cryptic, Peg," I said, trying not to sound defensive. "I'm following up."

Give it up, Peg.

She lifted her hands off the table in a manner I interpreted as "I was just asking. Don't shoot."

I'd been frustrated with Jenny B. for being light on the details and here I was doing the same thing, which was all I could do at this point. Before Jenny B. left for the day, I'd peppered her with questions about the mystery caller.

"Did anything come up on the caller ID? And you're sure you didn't catch a name? Did the call have a bad connection? Was it hard to hear her?"

Jenny B. had managed to decipher the woman saying that her sister was missing and she believed her sister's husband could be involved. So why was the voicemail recording so poor?

"Uh-oh. You're scrunching. What's going on?" Ellen asked as she stood over my desk. She'd stayed behind in the news meeting, emerging five minutes after it ended and heading straight for me.

"I should be asking you that. You're the one who looks like the cat that swallowed the canary."

Ellen beamed, reminding me of less rocky days. "I've got good news!"

"What?"

"How would you like to fill in as the morning show anchor next week?"

I almost stopped breathing. *Anchor?* It had been a dream of mine for so long that I had finally forced myself to stop thinking about it, and hadn't in what? A year? Two, maybe?

"Okay, this wasn't the reaction I was going for." Ellen frowned.

Not the reaction you were going for? Did you have something to do with this, Ellen?

"I'm in shock!" I said, allowing the news to sink in. "I mean, whose idea was this? Why now?"

Ellen shifted uncomfortably between her feet. "It was mine, actually," she said.

It's nice to know that Ellen is still looking out for me.

"William Shelton is going to be out all next week, so when the subject of fill-in anchor came up, I threw your name out there. I thought you'd be thrilled."

It took a minute, but my brain finally made the connection. This was good news, great news even, and it could be the first step toward bigger and better things beyond Channel 8. I would be filling in for a man, which was also not the norm.

"No! I mean yes, I am!" I said. "It's something I've always wanted to do."

"That's what I thought," Ellen said. "And this way, you'll be able to ease into it."

Anchoring never struck me as harder than reporting, just different. The prevailing thought, in any industry, is that the highest-paying job is the hardest job. Newsroom interns believe that, as do the people watching at home. In journalism school, there was a heavy emphasis on reporting. And when I got into this business, it wasn't hard to see how the reporters on the street were doing the most backbreaking work and taking all the risks. But anchoring, especially at a local news station, was always viewed as the grand prize. Contrast that with anchors I had worked with who had amassed enough power to come in an hour before the newscast. Some chose to spend that hour in makeup criticizing the writing and producing and anything else that made them feel in control.

What always struck me as strange was the anchor who, while introducing a reporter covering a life-threatening cold snap, thought it wise to comment, "Sorry you ended up getting this assignment." Or "Looks like you pulled the short straw," adding laughter to their out-of-touch commentary. I once heard a local anchor toss to a reporter by asking if the dangerous high winds would die down soon, because her hair could not take much more of it. People were losing power, trees were down, and the anchorman, sitting comfortably and safely inside the studio, was making hair jokes.

"Don't get me wrong. I'm excited! This is great, Ellen! Thank you!" I said, giving her the level of enthusiasm she was aiming for. "It's just so unexpected. Like, wow!"

There was a part of me that wished she had asked me first. But there likely wasn't time. When these opportunities came up, they tended to be settled quickly, at the speed of news. I knew that.

"So, are we talking for the entire week? Or just one day?" I asked when it suddenly occurred to me that anchoring would mean getting pulled off the crime unit.

Weren't you just complaining you were bored an hour ago?

Anchoring for a week would break up my routine, and I could still keep tabs on any percolating assignments.

"Well, yeah. Just for that week," she said. "Look, it's only Monday. If you need time to think about it—"

"No! I don't need time. Yes! I'll do it!"

"Ah . . . that's, that's . . . awesome, Jordan," Ellen said. "I can't wait to tell Peter. You know, this could be the start of something big."

I knew that Ellen was alluding to the main anchor chair. Was that what she really wanted for me? I was no longer sure myself whether anchoring was still a priority. I would love the salary upgrade. I'd be able to afford a full jar of that face cream instead of bootlegging samples. But could I be a voice for the voiceless sitting in that chair?

Ellen appeared relieved and satisfied. Her mission was accomplished. With our relationship ups and downs, it was no secret why she had pitched me as fill-in anchor and why she felt so good about it now. Though I doubted that she, for one minute, considered how the whole Justice Jordan image had been playing out in my mind. Now that I'd had a chance to think about it, this fill-in anchor assignment was less of an opportunity for me and more of a chance for the station to benefit from my growing popularity. They paid me, so they had that right, I supposed. *Just don't make it seem like you're doing me any favors.*

8

Tuesday, March 17

As eventfully as yesterday had begun, with Jenny B.'s urgent text message, it ended with a thud. That each day offered up a headline-grabbing opportunity was another misconception about the media that even my own mother, the crime buff, hadn't fully grasped after all these years. "What did you work on today? Were you the lead?" she often asked on her weekly check-in calls.

To stay busy and in the loop, I'd worked out a deal with the station that allowed me to cohost one of the popular radio shows, *Get Up with Gil*, on Tuesdays and Thursdays from eight to eleven A.M. I'd gotten to know Gil Thompson quite well over the years but only recently enjoyed the benefit of standing in proximity to the light and positive energy he cast over a South Side community for which he was a stalwart and trusted voice of the people. Our friendship started off in an odd fashion, with his sending over a bouquet of flowers my first week on the air. The flowers didn't turn into the date he'd wanted but forged the bonds of a friendship. It's funny how those first few months on air revealed a peculiar ritual for the newest reporter or anchor in town. A gaggle of people swooped in like migrating geese— some to try and get a date; others to solicit you to join this group or that one. There are, of course, the well-intentioned, who simply want to welcome you but also recognize that having your support for their annual 5K walk/run or charity auction would be a game changer. So they try to snag you when you're on the rise, as opposed to all the jaded veteran reporters, who no longer see the value in donating their free time to a good cause.

My role on *Get Up with Gil* was equal parts journalist and therapist. I could expect at least one caller per segment to lay down their testimony, then ask me, "What should I do? Where can I go?" And Gil would ask me the question I often dreaded. The following morning, about midway through the broadcast, on cue, he laid it on me.

"What are you working on these days?" he said, unintentionally setting expectations for our listening audience I couldn't meet. What could possibly sustain the persona of justice seeker that I now embodied? What's more, you're only as important and as relevant as your last story. This of course is an industry truism, but for me it was a constant source of inner conflict now that I was an enterprise reporter who only focused on the lead investigative stories.

As I considered my answer, I adjusted the heavy oversize headphones that always felt as though they were sliding off my ears. Then a light went on. I did in fact have some news to share.

"Well, Gil, starting Monday, I'll be filling in as co-anchor on the morning broadcast," I said.

Gil's producer, perched behind a glassed-in booth, punched the "oohs and aahs" track.

"Oh, so that means when we go to dinner, it's on you." Gil laughed.

What is this? The Dating Game *now?*

"That's exciting!" Gil said.

It is. Isn't it?

"Yes," I said, trying to sound convinced. "It's a dream come true. I'm looking forward to it."

"Just for a week, though?" he asked.

"Yes, just a week," I confirmed.

I figured I also might as well mention a couple of speaking engagements in the community I had coming up. There had been an uptick in these of late. Since the promo started running, I'd received invitations from several women's and victims' organizations who asked me to come in to talk about the media and police handling of crimes that affect Black and brown communities and female victims.

"You never stop. You stay busy," Gil said.

"If you're not busy, you're not a boss," I said.

"Oohh!" Gil, shocked by my reply, brought his fist to his mouth and tilted so far back in his chair I thought he'd fall out. It's always surprising to people when they hear me speak outside of television. Some are emboldened by my candor to take a leap and try and forge a connection. Gil's listeners were among this group.

"The phone lines are open! What's on your mind, Chicago? Call and let us know. 773-555-1300. Who's our first caller?"

"It's your girl, Belinda," said the producer, from the adjacent room.

Oh no. Belinda Brackley. She was a frequent caller, a self-appointed grist master of the rumor mill and wannabe reporter. I had been meaning to ask Gil if the station paid for her unverified, unsubstantiated "reports" or permitted her space to practice her hobby for the sheer entertainment value.

"Good morning, Gil baby," Belinda said with a hint of flirta-tion. "How're you doing?"

"Aw! It's my good friend, Belinda 'I got the scoop' Brackley! Good morning to you, sis."

"Hey, Jordan," she said flatly.

"Hi, Belinda," I said, straining to sound cheerful.

"You got a scoop for me?" Gil asked.

"You know I do," she replied proudly. "You heard about that murder at the Civic Opera House, right?"

"Yeah, man," Gil said. "I hate stories like this. Listen, broth-ers and sisters, no relationship is worth killing somebody over. Okay? If somebody falls out of love with you, just move on."

"It's easier than doing hard time," I chimed in.

"I know that's right," Gil agreed.

"And now he faces an additional charge of second-degree assault for assaulting his public defender," I said.

"I saw that!" Gil said. "That was insane, right?"

"I know. I was there. I saw it. Her head barely missed the end of that table. If she'd hit that, it could've killed her."

"And those are some big ol' sturdy wooden tables, too," Gil said.

"Right. At a minimum, she could have been seriously in-jured," I said.

"Well, I heard he was seeing somebody, too," Belinda inter-rupted. "That relationship had long been over. Their divorce was almost final."

"Wait a minute. What?" Gil asked, feigning utter shock.

"Yeah, she knew about his side piece. It wasn't no secret. He's the one who stepped out on her. Okay? It wasn't about that doctor. It was about the business."

"What business?" I asked.

"They owned a business together, a bodega down the street from the gym where Guillermo used to work out. A friend of mine works out there, too, and he told me they got behind on their sales taxes, but she's the one who came up with the money to pay 'em, and so the judge awarded her the store. Did you know *that*, Jordan?"

"Well . . . no. I-I'm not covering the story," I stammered, offering an explanation that many of our viewers, I knew, wouldn't be able to fully grasp. "It's not an investigation, so I'm not on the story anymore."

"Oh?" she said, a little overbearing. "Well, the news media is trying to make it sound like a love triangle. But it wasn't about that. She got the store and full custody of the kids. Police were at their house all the time. They say he used to beat on her, but I heard she was the one beating on him. He snapped over the business. That doctor just got in the way."

I felt nauseous knowing that some people would believe her unchecked report as the gospel truth.

"How can you be so sure, Belinda?" I challenged her. "I mean, this is hearsay, and very dangerous, I might add."

"Then why don't you check it out yourself," she pushed back.

"Whether I do or don't, it doesn't change the fact that two people are dead. And frankly, I'm not comfortable with your painting this victim as somehow deserving what happened to her. You shouldn't put stuff out there you can't back up."

"Oh, I can back it up!"

I shot Gil a look and gestured as if I was hanging up a telephone receiver, mouthing the words "this is over," and swiped my hand across my neck.

"All right, Belinda with the scoop. What y'all think? 773-555-1300."

"Gil! One more thing. I want to tell your listeners to follow me on Facebook and Twitter @TheScoopwithBelinda. Spell *with* out, okay? The. Scoop. With. Belinda."

"Okay, Belinda. I've got you. Who's our next caller?"

Are reporter wannabes on social media sites my competition now? I mentally checked out for the rest of the show. Afterward, Gil asked, "Wanna grab some breakfast?"

"I wish I could, but I've gotta get to the newsroom," I said as I passed the receptionist desk on the way out.

"Hey, Jordan, hold up," she said. "I took a few messages while you were on the air."

She peeled one off from the stack. "You should take a look at this one."

Please call. Urgent. Missing person. Shelly Biltmore 219-555-4389.

Instinctively I knew. It was the same woman from before. *At last.*

9

Starving as usual, all I could think about on the way back to the station was stopping by the new Asian fusion restaurant, Sushi Samurai, that opened in the building on the ground floor. Apparently, I wasn't the only one who missed breakfast, because by eleven-thirty, a line had already formed and spilled out into the main lobby. I didn't have time to wait, not if I wanted to enjoy my food and make the news meeting in the next thirty minutes. I had no problem playing the "best customer" card to jump the line and place my order.

Hey, Cessily, it's me, Jordan, I texted. Are you working? Can I ask you for a favor?

Hey, Jordan. Sure, what can I do for you?

Just as I read her text, I saw Cessily come out of the side metal door to the kitchen. The stress of the late-morning rush was etched in her forehead.

"Hey, Cess. I've got a meeting to get to. Can you squeeze me in?"

"It'll probably still be close to fifteen minutes." She frowned apologetically.

"That's perfect! I'll have the usual. I'm gonna grab a table by the window. It'd be great if I could pay for it now to save time."

"Okay, I'll bring the check right over."

"Thanks, Cess, you're a lifesaver."

She started to walk away but whipped back around. "Oh, I almost forgot," she said. "I have something to tell you. See you in a sec."

I planted myself at a small two-top table in the corner near a window facing the Wrigley Building. I pulled my iPad from my bag but hadn't time to sign on before Cessily stepped from behind the counter and headed over to me with the bill and sat down.

"So what is it you want to tell me?" I asked.

I was about to answer when the blaring sound of two fire trucks interrupted my train of thought. *I wonder where they're headed?* Cessily leaned in with her elbows on the table. "When we first opened this morning, a woman stopped by here looking for you."

"Here? What'd she want?"

"No idea, but one of our bussers and a kitchen staffer told me she asked whether you ever came in here."

"And this happened today? I must've just missed her."

Cessily nodded.

"Today and apparently yesterday, too," she said.

"They get a name?"

She shook her head.

"What'd she look like?" I asked.

"They said she had bright red hair. From the way they described her, it sounded like she'd be hard to miss."

"Any idea what she wanted?"

"Nope. They just said she was asking about you and they saw her hanging around the lobby after."

"Hmm, well, thanks for the heads-up," I said, and handed her my credit card.

"Be careful, Jordan. It sounds kind of creepy."

"Oh, I've dealt with worse. But thanks. Will you call me if she comes back though?"

"Sure. Will do. I'll be right back with your card."

More and more I wondered whether the whole Justice Jordan shtick was worth the risk. I scanned the restaurant and thought about getting up to look out into the lobby but then thought better of it. If she was lying in wait, I could walk right into her trap.

A few minutes later, Cessily sent over a server with my order and credit card. With less than fifteen minutes to spare, I scanned the lobby but didn't see anyone who matched this woman's description. Then just as I was about to head toward the elevators, I felt a tight grip and a tug on my left arm that made me stumble backward.

"What the hell?" I yanked my arm loose and regained my footing. I spun around, and there she was. The redhead. I immediately understood why the restaurant workers described her as hard to miss. It was so fiery it couldn't have been her natural color, with about an inch shaved down to her scalp above her ear on the right side.

"Jordan? Oh my god, I'm so sorry. I didn't mean to grab you like that. I-I just couldn't let you leave. I've *got* to talk to you. It's life-or-death."

Her voice sounded gruff. It reminded me of two pieces of sandpaper rubbing together. Her clothes, a mauve-colored pants suit with a plain white T-shirt underneath, seemed more like an attempt to mask everything else she was giving off, like she was trying to appear to be someone else.

"Excuse me! Who are you? What do you want?"

She was a woman on the verge of a breakdown and not hiding it very well.

"I'm Shelly Biltmore. I've been trying to get in touch with you. It's about my sister. She's missing and I think her husband did something to her."

Oh my god!

"Hey, you called the hotline yesterday. Why'd you hang up?" I asked.

"Yes! Yes! That was me. I'm so sorry. But the police were trying to reach me as soon as they transferred my call to you. And I had to see what they had to say, and after that, I . . . I . . ."

She burst into tears. Her back and shoulders now visibly shaking, she planted her face in her hands. I looked around the lobby, panicked by the scene she was making.

"Somebody's gotta do something!" she screamed. "I need help!"

"All right. But listen, this isn't the way to get it. Now get control of yourself."

"Nobody's listening," she continued. "I've tried everything!"

"Okay! I'm listening, but you've got to calm down. Let's go back inside the restaurant and sit down. All right?"

Shelly nodded and I gestured toward her to lead the way. "You first." There was no way I wanted this woman walking behind me after what she just pulled. I caught Cessily's eye as we walked back into Sushi Samurai and nodded toward Shelly. Cessily nodded back, affirming that this was indeed the same woman who'd asked about me earlier.

The table by the window had been taken, but I found two seats in the back next to the washroom. "Let's sit here, Shelly," I said. The bad lighting in the lobby masked features that were now coming into view. She picked up a napkin off the table and patted her cheeks and eyes. That's when I noticed the tattoos on her hand.

I gestured to one of the waitstaff walking by. "Can you bring her a glass of water, please?"

I should have opened with "You know, this is completely un-orthodox. We have a process for sharing news tips and infor-mation. And this ain't it." But her whole body appeared to be shaking. It was hard to know whether it was from angst, fear, or embarrassment. But clearly she was struggling to keep it together, and now was not the time. Instead, I asked, "Where are you from?"

She closed her eyes. "Indiana. A farming community just outside Rensselaer. It's about an hour and a half from here."

"You drove all the way to Chicago to talk to me? Why didn't you just call back?"

"I'd already called so many times and I could tell they were tired of me or thought I was crazy. And then when I finally got through, I had to go talk to the police. I just thought, at this point, I'd do better just coming here."

I thought back on the news article Ellen found out of India-napolis. "Rensselaer? Is your sister named Marla?"

"Yes! You've heard about her disappearance?"

"I saw a story on the wire yesterday. But the article was at least three weeks old," I said.

"What's the wire?" she asked.

"Just a place where you can find stories from all over."

"Okay. Well, anyway, look, you wanna know why I drove all the way here yesterday? It's because of the sheriff's office. Those bastards called and told me they were calling off the search."

"Why?"

"Because they said she used her credit card the day before at a convenience store in Chicago, but the cameras weren't working. Makes no sense. For one thing, her husband cut off all her credit cards after she left with the kids."

"Did she have a debit card? Maybe that's what they meant."

"I don't care what kind of card it was. There's no way Marla dropped off her kids and just took off! No fucking way!"

The more upset Shelly got, the clearer her persona came into focus. She reminded me of the type of woman guys felt comfortable around. She was attractive but gave off a drinking buddy vibe.

"Shelly, I know you're upset. But the credit card usage, that…" I trailed off as I tried to choose my next words carefully.

"What?" Shelly asked, growing impatient.

"To them, the fact that her card was used suggests she's on the move and doesn't want to be found."

Shelly shook her head.

"I know it's hard," I continued, "but you may have to consider that Marla did in fact just take off."

She didn't like me saying that at all. Her lips tightened. I wouldn't put it past her to try and take a swing at me. I eased back in my chair just in case.

"You don't know my sister," she said through gritted teeth.

"Well, I mean, I know you're—"

"My sister is the kindest, most loving mother I've ever seen," she interrupted. "She left that asshole because she is a good mother."

"Shelly, I understand it might feel and look that way to you. But in this business, I've learned that a person you think you know can do unfathomable things."

She looked down at the table and rubbed her forehead.

Maybe I am going about this all wrong. Back up, Jordan, and just listen.

"Look, I'm sorry. I'm not trying to draw any conclusions from the little information I have to go on. Just tell me, in your words, what you believe happened to Marla."

Shelly picked up the water glass and took a sip. "How much time do you got?"

10

The more Shelly talked about her sister's failed marriage, the more worked up she became. The man she described didn't have one redeeming quality.

"What's his name? What does he do for a living?" I asked her.

"Jim. She calls him Jimmy," she said, the look of disgust not something she was remotely interested in masking from me. "He's a construction contractor. It's the family's business. He works for his dad, but I've never seen or heard of him going in for more than an hour here and there. Most of the time he's at home, playing video games. The minute my sister asks for help with the kids, he suddenly has to rush to a worksite or something in his office needs his attention. He's a lousy parent and husband."

"So I take it you have a low opinion of your brother-in-law."

"Oh, you have no idea," she said. "He's always putting her down about her weight. She had a hard time after their second child, Dara, was born."

"What do you mean?"

"She had the baby blues. You've heard of that?"

I nodded.

"I told her if she'd stayed on the farm and worked the horses with me, that baby weight woulda come right off her."

"You have stables?" I asked. That would partly explain what

I'd already noticed. Her hands were rough and dry, as if the sun had burned her skin to a raw red on some days.

"Yep, and three hundred acres of farmland, too. Our family has owned unincorporated land in Jasper County for forty years. Me and Marla worked the farm practically our whole lives, until she got married and moved away. My only break was the two and a half years I worked full-time as a stable hand in Greenwood. After my father died, I dedicated most of my time to the farm again."

"I grew up in Texas. My aunt and uncle had a farm with a few horses."

I knew that playing into the "everyone in Texas has a horse" cliché was unwise, but I wanted to form a bond, build a connection. A trick of the trade.

"You ride English or Western?"

Busted. I had been on a horse maybe five times in my life. One of those was a frail old horse at my cousin's birthday party, and even that frightened me.

"Western, actually," I said, trying to sound confident in my answer and grateful that Shelly nodded her approval and moved on.

"It's hard work. These hands aren't the only casualties," she said, holding them up in front of her face, seeming more comfortable now that there'd been an explanation. "You oughta see all the bruises I've gotten from being kicked."

While I could appreciate this lighter moment between us, time was ticking, and the conversation was getting derailed. "So, Shelly, back to Jim. Why'd she leave him?"

"Because Jim is an asshole. It started after she had their second child. As I said, he was always riding her about losing weight and putting her down. He was abusive, emotionally, and I have a feeling it might have escalated."

"To physical abuse?"

Anguish crept over her face. Shelly stared down at the table, her mouth drawn tight.

"Did you ever see any scars or bruises?"

"With her living over three hundred miles away, I never had any proof. But I know my sister."

"Did you ask her if he'd put hands on her?"

She shook her head. "Even if I had asked her, she would have denied it. Marla wanted everybody to think she was living this ideal life. But something changed in the last two years."

Ah. The ideal life fantasy. I know it well.

Shelly's mood turned remorseful. If I had been checking reactions off on one of those feelings charts teachers use to help preschoolers acknowledge their emotions, Shelly's would have been full.

"Marla used to bring the kids around me over Thanksgiving or the Christmas holiday. That stopped two years ago."

Shelly's eyes were red and puffy from what I gathered was the result of many bouts of crying in the weeks since Marla vanished. Her arms resting on the table, hands clasped tightly in front of her. It was then that the depth of Shelly's pain came into focus for me. This wasn't just stress over her sister's disappearance but a festering wound that took her back to a pain from her past.

"I asked her to let the kids stay for the summer, you know, to grow up as we did with the fresh air and space to run around and be kids. But she said no, and I—well, frankly, it shocked me. I don't think she made that decision. I believe he was isolating her."

Or maybe he didn't want his children around someone who hated his guts.

"Please don't get upset, but I have to ask. Was there any cheating going on . . . on either side?"

Surprisingly, Shelly seemed to welcome the question. She sat up taller in her seat. "He definitely was cheating. Marla didn't have time to cheat. She poured her whole self into those kids."

"How do you know for sure?"

"Marla told me he started staying out late, and eventually there'd be nights he wouldn't come home at all."

"Did she have any proof?" I asked.

"What else would a married man be doing out all night?"

"Did she confront him about her suspicions?"

"I don't know."

"How long ago did she leave?"

My rapid-fire questions rescued Shelly momentarily from her painful recollections.

"It'd been about four months since she moved back home from Danville when she disappeared."

Each time Shelly uttered the word *missing* or *disappeared* in reference to her sister, torment flashed across her face like lightning in the clouds. She buried her face in her hands again for a moment before she was able to pull it together, then wiped her tears with the back of her hand.

"Okay," she said more to herself than me. "This hurts."

I kept going. She didn't come all this way to be coy. "How'd she meet her husband?"

"She and her best friend from high school went to San Diego for a quick getaway the weekend of the air show at the Marine Corps air station. She said it was a nice change of scenery. Jim loves air shows and I think that is, like, the largest one."

"It is," I interjected. "One of the largest, I mean. I went my senior year in college for the weekend."

I was dating Lin at the time, and he dragged me to the Miramar Air Show. It was a whirlwind trip. He took me on a tour of the naval base there. He was so proud being able to finally demonstrate to me the power and might of the Navy and the Pacific Fleet Surface Force. It all validated why he said he wanted a career in the military despite the regular interrogation from friends and family wanting to know why. I admired his passion. Fell deeper in love with him because of it, believing, at the time, that he would at the very least accept, if not admire, the passion I had for my work, too.

"They met that weekend," Shelly continued. "They happened to be staying at the same hotel and they met at the bar. By the time she came back home, Marla told me and everyone who would listen that he was going to be her husband."

"How old was Marla when they met?"

"She was twenty-four, I think. I remember her birthday was coming up. They married about a year later. But I'll be honest with you, I don't think she was that in love with him. I think she saw him as a ticket out of Rensselaer. It's too rural for her. Too slow. Danville, Kentucky, isn't exactly New York or Beverly Hills, but it's a step up at least from Rensselaer. If you are looking for a faster life."

I was just shy of my twenty-first birthday at the air show. Marla and I quite possibly attended the same year. That would be some coincidence.

"Jim's family is well known in Danville," she continued. "Marla felt like he could provide her with a good life."

There it was. What Shelly described was starting to sound all too familiar. Marla married into what she perceived as a better situation. She'd gone looking for it and she found it. The grand prize. For some women, moving the decimal point to the right in their bank balance, plus a couple of extra bedrooms and a two-car garage, was all they needed to get to "I do." But how many of those situations ended in divorce and betrayal?

"Did your sister work?" I asked, instantly sorry I'd referenced her in the past tense. "In Danville, I mean."

"She worked before she had kids. She's a stay-at-home mom now," Shelly said, using the present tense. "She's always the first to decorate the house for every holiday. You should see their house for Halloween. It's ridiculous! The kids have the best birthday gift bags for guests I've ever seen. I mean it's *her* kid's birthday and she sends all the other kids home with gifts. Who does that?"

"So did you ever go visit her and the kids in Danville?"

Shelly sighed deeply and rubbed her forehead, as if she was bracing for a migraine.

"What?"

"I'm just thinking about the last time I was there. That visit didn't end well."

"Tell me about it."

"My nephew Cameron called and told me his mom and dad were fighting—like, a lot. So I drove up to Danville one afternoon, unannounced. I was afraid if I'd asked to come, she would've said no."

"Why would you think that? Weren't you close?"

"We were, but . . . I don't know. Marla was acting different. It had gone on for a while. She wasn't opening up to me like she had in the past. Anyway, I drove up there, and she seemed like she was glad to see me. We had a great time that first day. We even drove out to Louisville and took the kids to Six Flags."

"Just you and Marla? Or did Jim go with you?"

"No, it was just us and the kids. She seemed happy. Relaxed."
She smiled. "Her little one, Dara—I used to tease Marla, I told
her, 'Dara clings to you like a koala bear.' That was my nickname for her."

"Koala?"

Shelly nodded. "She was so adorable that day. There's nothing sweeter than those tiny hands around your neck and those
little candy kisses when she's chomping down on a Dum-Dum
sucker."

It was apparent that Shelly really loved those kids. I knew
the satisfaction those relationships could bring and have always
said that so long as I have the love of my nieces and nephews
and my youngest cousin, Drucilla, I didn't need to have children
of my own.

"Okay, but you said it didn't end well. What changed?"

"My nephew and I have a special bond. It's hard to describe,
but I told Marla I think Cam was supposed to be my kid; angels
delivered him to the wrong address."

I nodded, understanding as the aunt without a child how
that must have felt for her. "What happened next?"

"Cam and I were in his room sitting on the floor. He was
showing me a model airplane he was building. He's got a gift
for building and putting things together. I asked him how
school was going, and he got really serious all of a sudden."

"How so?"

"He said, 'Aunt Shell, when I'm at school, all I can hear is
them yelling,' and he started to cry."

I had experienced that feeling of helplessness as a child, listening to my parents go at it, and there was nothing I could do
but stay out of grown folks' business. I never judged them for

it. My aunts and uncles argued, too. So did my friends' parents. I learned early on that passions were ignited at both ends of a relationship, just in different ways.

"Cam told me they mostly fought at night and in the car."

What's special about the car?

She chimed in as if she had read my mind. "I blame it on proximity. Someone's getting on your nerves, it's worse the closer they are to you," she said. "That's a pretty big house, but the kids' rooms sit between the master bedroom and the guest room. Dara's room is right next door to her mom and dad's and Cam's is directly across the hall from hers. That long hallway carries sound pretty well, because later that night, when they started in on each other, I could hear them, too."

"How bad was it?"

"It was bad, Jordan." Shelly shook her head.

"Could you tell what they were fighting about?"

Shelly shifted in the chair.

"I don't know what started it, but Jim just kept saying, 'Did you find what you were looking for, Marla? Did you? Did you?' God! He would not let it go. It was irritating, to say the least."

"What do you mean?"

"Him always repeating himself," she said; even now recalling what he said was clearly frustrating for her. "It's like an intimidation tactic, I think. His way of belittling you."

"Anybody or just Marla?"

"*Any*body."

Shelly was right; it was a tactic. Textbook abuse.

"Marla screamed, 'Get away from me!' And right after, something shattered. I mean, I thought to myself, *That was more than a glass*. It made this huge sound. A door slammed and Jim started cursing, calling her crazy and saying he's had enough."

"I'm sure the kids didn't sleep through all that," I said.

"No," she said, shaking her head. "When I came out into the hallway, their bedroom doors were cracked open. They looked terrified. Cam and I locked eyes, and I told them both to go back into their rooms and Aunt Shell would see what was going on. Jim was still yelling when I knocked on the door, threatening to call the cops. I banged on the door harder and asked if Marla was okay. He yelled, 'Go away, Shelly! Mind your own business!' Finally I screamed at the top of my lungs, 'Jim, open this fucking door!'"

"Wait, Jim was threatening to call the cops?" I asked.

If Jim was abusing Marla, why would he threaten to call the cops?

"He finally opened the door but not enough for me to see. He was as red as a beet and there was a little blood on his forehead."

"Blood?"

"Yeah. Not a lot, just a stream that stopped by his right eye."

"It sounds like they got into a physical altercation?"

"Yeah, I think he came at her, and she fought back."

If he was bleeding, then what shape was Marla in?

"There was no way I was leaving her alone with that monster so he could come after her again."

"And Marla? Was she hurt?"

"I couldn't see her at first, but I could hear her. She told Jim to let me in, but he refused. I'll never forget the way he looked at me with that smirky little mouth of his and said, 'I can't wait for you to leave. Why are you even here? You're not welcome.' I warned him one last time that he had better open that door."

"Then what?"

"He tried to close it on me, but I charged with all my strength, Jordan, and I knocked him back on his heels and he almost tumbled onto the bed."

My first impression of Shelly was correct. She was scrappy.

"Wow. So this got really ugly," I said. "Where was Marla?"

"She was in the bathroom in her bathrobe. The shower was running, and it was all steamy in there. I was about to go to her, but she stopped me because I wasn't wearing shoes. I looked down, and sure enough, there were large chunks of glass scattered about. It looked like it was a vase."

"The thick, heavy kind," I said.

"Exactly," she said, the word coming as she tilted her head and nodded affirmatively. "So, I stepped over the glass and went to her. I asked if she was hurt and if she wanted me to call the police, and Jim was like, 'Be my guest. Call the police.'"

"Did Marla have any marks on her?"

"None that I could see," she said.

"Did Marla throw that vase at Jim?"

Shelly hesitated. "Yes, she did. Like I said, he was coming at her."

"She could've killed him," I said matter-of-factly, to which Shelly offered neither response nor rebuttal.

"So Marla wasn't hurt?"

Shelly shook her head.

"And the police weren't called?"

"No."

"How'd it all end that night?" I asked.

"It ended with Marla telling me to go home."

Shelly's shoulders quaked and she started to cry. Something snapped at that moment. It was so palpable, I could almost hear a tear.

"It was, like, our connection, this emotional tether that we could rely on to pull the other closer when we needed to, was suddenly severed, and she just floated away."

"How'd that make you feel?"

"Betrayed."

Shelly's shoulders slumped and she stared at the floor. The pain was fresh.

"What happened after you left?"

"I didn't see her for almost two years. She'd send pictures of her and the kids. Cam, he's eight now, but he's a pretty good shot with those throwaways," Shelly said, forcing a smile.

"Why do you think she stayed away like that?"

"I pushed her too hard, I think."

"Pushed her how?"

"Pushed her to leave him. Maybe that wasn't the right way to go about it. People used to say it's a fool who gets between a married couple. They'll fight like cats and dogs and get mad at you for saying something," Shelly said. "But now I know better. That's the old way of thinking."

My grandmother used to say something similar, but I didn't admit that to Shelly as she carried on with accepting the blame.

"Walking away meant leaving an entire life behind, you know? I made it sound easy. It wasn't. I've never been married, so what do I know? She was so wrapped up in the kids and their activities. She even volunteered as an assistant coach for Cam's soccer team. She played in high school, but since she became a mom, she wasn't athletic at all. She gave a hundred percent of herself to everybody else."

People toss out that adage as a compliment, but nobody gives a hundred percent to everybody else. That would defy human nature.

11

Are u coming to the mtg?

Ellen sent that text message twenty minutes ago, but I could see through the conference room's tinted glass that the meeting hadn't started yet. I'm convinced the only thing that starts on time in a newsroom is the newscast. Every minute seems to come with the necessary gossip and awkward chitchat I would rather avoid. I didn't mind coming in late. Those minutes leading up to the actual start of assignments being issued and the unpacking of stories being pursued can be brutal. Way too much phony small talk about weekend plans and kids and, perish the thought, the incessant inquiries about my dating life. The last "let's investigate Jordan's personal life" round had worn on my nerves, but now with all the new attention I was getting, it was even more grating.

I'll sit right here with my teriyaki bowl, thank you.

Even when the meeting started late, Ellen enforced strict time limits to ensure it ended on time. Otherwise, those meetings could stretch longer than the traffic on the Kennedy Expressway to O'Hare Airport. Perhaps, like me, she'd grown weary of reporters who liked to hear themselves talk and producers angling for attention. It also struck me early on how lonely some of these people must be when they were away from the newsroom. Years of investing in building a career had limited their time for family and friends. Work was all-consuming and fulfilling, up to a point. Viewers might imagine that we are friends, but at the end of the day, we don't have dinner or drinks together. Some well-known anchors go home and spend their evenings with wine and recordings of the newscast. Watching it over and over, studying how they read a story or how the person next to them appeared to be mugging for the camera when the wide lens showed them side by side.

Not me. I wasn't up for it in general. Today I needed this to be in and out. My mind was still restless after my conversation with Shelly.

Had I overpromised by telling her that I would call the local police and reporters to get their take on the case? Do I want to get involved with this woman?

If I'd told her there was nothing I could do, how would she have reacted? If I was being honest with myself, my curiosity might have had more to do with my response than Shelly or even her sister. Was I feeling the pressure to land the next big lead story? Was the taste of attention and seeing the ratings pop intoxicating? Or was this a chance to stretch my investigative chops outside of Channel 8's boundaries? The Jackson Five sang about going back to Indiana, yet clearly those weren't the same feelings shared by Marla Hancock. According to her sister, Marla couldn't wait to get out of Rensselaer.

After fifteen minutes or so, I noticed people flowing out of the conference room.

Ellen headed straight for me. "Where were you?" she asked.

Was I now *expected* to attend? Just as I was about to ask her what happened in the meeting, I realized I didn't care. All I could think about now was what happened to Marla Hancock.

Her sister had described a woman who, even before devoting her life to marriage and children, had been the rock of her family. A nurturer.

"After our mom died, I became so . . . self-destructive," Shelly said. "I couldn't've gotten through that without Marla."

"You got Sushi Samurai without me?" Ellen teased.

"It's a long story. Ellen, I'm freaked out. I was on my way upstairs before the meeting when this woman grabbed me by the arm and said she had to talk to me."

"What? Are you okay? What do you mean, she grabbed you?"

"No, no, not like that. She's the caller. Remember? From yesterday? The story you pulled up on the wire about the missing Indiana woman. It was her sister."

Ellen set down the folder she was carrying and, with a great bit of drama, threw up both of her hands.

"Wait. What? Slow down. Does she want you to interview her?"

I knew what Ellen was getting at, and I was loath to tread into waters only for her to tell me I couldn't swim. "Nope. Believe it or not, she didn't come here asking to be interviewed," I said.

"What did she come here for, then?" Ellen asked.

"She knows the police aren't going to care until she can prove her sister is missing. She's not going to be our lead story. Someone has to prove something happened first," I said.

Who am I trying to convince? Ellen or myself?

I spoke with the voice of reason, but in my mind, I knew that Shelly wanted me to help her prove that Marla was not only missing but a victim. As genuinely crushed as she seemed to be today, Shelly was also extremely sharp.

"Ellen, she doesn't think her sister is missing. I believe deep down, she thinks she's dead."

"What'd you tell her?"

"I listened, that's all," I said. "She was hysterical at first. I had to calm her down." I didn't answer Ellen's questions directly on purpose.

"Wait, does she live in Chicago? Is she from here? What's the tie?"

What was the tie? A woman was missing, and her sister didn't believe she just took off. I reared back to make sure the person I was looking at was the Ellen I knew.

"Listen, Jordan, if you want to look into it, fine. But you know as much as I do," she said, leaning close to my ear, "that if we give any airtime to this story without some meat on the bones, it'll just look like we care about this missing person case because she's a white woman."

12

Once I'm onto something, I am compelled to see it through. Loose ends equal lost sleep. It has been that way for me since the beginning. While I was working in a small news market in Texas, my first TV gig right out of college, my news director at the time told me in a heart-to-heart that these little markets are weed-out classes. It's here that you learn whether you are cut out for this business and create the blueprint for the type of reporter you will be for the rest of your career. I quit before they could fire me, and just as the words *weed out* had become my reality, something right out of a movie changed it all.

Unemployed and convinced that this was not the career for me, I had already paid to attend a journalism convention in Houston and was not willing to waste the registration fee. At a forum on how reporters save and change lives, I met the local news anchor I grew up watching as a kid. All these years later, Madge Green was exactly the same as she appeared each night when my dad and I would bond over the five o'clock news, debating the lead story and yelling at the always wrong weatherman. She was petite, and when I saw her in person, I realized that she was very thin. The red tweed jacket she wore that day, I was certain, was the same one I saw her wear on the air. Her cropped blond bob with never a strand out of place made her appear approachable, not rigid or caricatural. From the waist down, a view concealed by the anchor desk, she was in dark boyfriend jeans that screamed "I don't do this look often, but I want to appear cool." Madge was a local legend, and though she was coiffed to anchor perfection, she still gave off an "I smoke cigarettes and will have a drink with you after work" kind of vibe. I knew she was from Ohio, because she constantly referred to the state on air, especially during football season. She always gave the Ohio State team a shout-out during her banter with the local sports guys. After the panel, I went over and introduced myself. There was an instant connection. I cannot explain it, but it was enough that she invited me to visit the station anytime. A week later, I took her up on the offer and spent the day shadowing her. While in the cafeteria, the GM, Jeff Tramble, came over to say hi to Madge. She was so proud to introduce me as her mentee. Madge was part of a wave of powerful woman anchors in the late 1990s who were inspired by Barbara Walters. Hard work was paying off in the form of visibility and agency, and Madge was determined to open the door for other women. I am not sure whether Jeff Tramble knew what was happening, but before I could speak, Madge steamrolled him and said, "You must see her tape."

Madge later shared that she stalled him for twenty minutes with random topics to give me time to run to my car and come back. I remember Tramble's reaction to the cold résumé tape being forced into his hand.

"You don't waste an opportunity, do you?" he said.

How I went from wanting to leave the business to this moment, I could never explain. But a month later, I signed a three-year contract to report at my dad's go-to news channel. Interestingly, after I got the job, Madge and I didn't socialize or even talk much in the office. I believe she didn't want anyone to think I hadn't earned my spot, and any closeness with her would have given that storyline air to become the truth. Just a token hire.

• •

Facebook was like an open invitation to the world to "Come find me." All I had to do was enter an email address, create a password, and upload a profile picture. Voilà! I was now part of a virtual community. But I didn't come here for friends; I came here to follow my suspicions that Marla's disappearance and the breakup of her marriage were inextricably linked. Ellen was right, though. If a news station ninety miles away began following the story more closely than the local media, it could be perceived as another case of missing white woman syndrome. Five years ago, that term was coined by a legendary broadcast journalist to describe the media frenzy that occurred whenever a white woman who fit a certain description, like a college student or a suburban mom, went missing. Curiously, that didn't seem to include Marla Hancock. *She was a white suburban mom. Where was the frenzy?*

I searched Marla's name and six Marla Hancock profiles popped up. Two were pictured alone; three were clearly not her. Marla was white, and the three remaining women were not. The one that was left had no profile picture. Just a photo of a sunset. I clicked on it, scrolled down to a list of tabs and selected "photos." I was sure I had found the right one when I came across a mosaic of images of kids playing soccer, with the team holding up a trophy in the center, captioned, "Cam, you did it!" I could see a resemblance between Marla and Shelly. They had the same oval-shaped face and a strong likeness around the eyes, both with deep upper lids and faint eyelashes. I clicked clumsily through Marla's page and landed on what appeared to be countless thumbnail pictures of Marla with her children at birthday parties, museums, or posing with their favorite toy. There was one of Marla, Jim, and their kids on Halloween. I thought back to what Shelly said about her sister going all out on the holidays, because they were doing the most to pull off a *Star Wars* theme. Marla, her long hair rolled into buns on either side of her head, was dressed as Princess Leia; Jim, clearly wearing a wig, posed as Han Solo; a younger Cam portrayed Darth Vader; and their daughter, a toddler perched on her mother's hip, completed the tableau as a baby Yoda, with a Binky in her mouth.

A few of the images fit into the life I imagined she lived now but also of her life before Jim and the kids. One showed a teenage Marla with another girl captioned "Homecoming." There was another of Marla and the same young woman posed in front of a statue of the mythological god Neptune, his torso jutting out of a stone base. It was hard to figure out where it was taken. I strained to see a sliver of beach and an ocean in the background. Oh wow! I knew precisely where this photo had been taken. Along the boardwalk at Virginia Beach. Lin was stationed there during my junior year in college. I let curiosity get the best of me. The search icon on the top right-hand corner of my screen challenged me, and I began to type: L-I-N . . .

Do I really want to know? Is he even on Facebook? Probably not. J-A-C-K . . .

But if he is, he shouldn't be hard to find.

S-O-N. I tapped enter, and this time, only one profile popped up. *The* one. Lin Jackson, with the words *lieutenant commander* behind his name in parentheses.

Wow. He made lieutenant commander. That's a big deal.

I scanned every detail of his face. Maturity had chiseled his round cheeks, but he was otherwise unchanged.

Really? You couldn't have done me the favor of losing your hair?

I scrolled apprehensively through his page, playing with fire. So far, so good. It was filled mostly with images of Navy life.

You can stop now, Jordan. Stop now.

I scrolled back to the top of the page and clicked on the word *photos.* Lin had many fewer of these than Marla had. I pulled up an image of Lin with his family at his parents' house at Christmas. I recognized the fireplace in the background and the Black Saint Nick statue his mother always made certain people could see.

Ah, look at his mom. Oh, my goodness, is that his little sister, Melody? She's all grown up. Hmm. Where's his dad? Oh no. I wonder if he passed away?

There was a beautiful little girl with a happy birthday tiara tipping off her head. She smiled broadly, the telltale missing front tooth that put her age at around five or six years old. She was holding on to Lin's leg.

Where's her mother? You know you should quit now, Jordan.

"Hey, Jordan, are you okay?"

I looked up to see executive producer Tracy Klein standing outside my cubicle, her expression worried.

"Oh, hi, Tracy. Yeah, yeah. I'm fine, I'm fine."

"Okay," she said apprehensively. "Bad day?"

"No, it's good. Weird but good," I said, and faked a laugh.

"All right. See ya later," she said.

"See ya."

I grabbed my cell phone and dialed Lisette.

"Hey, Jordie!"

"Hey, Liz, can you talk?" I said softly.

"Sure. Why are you whispering?"

"I'm at my desk. Girl, guess what?"

"What?"

"I found Lin on Facebook."

"Oh," she said. And then, in a more emphatic voice, "Oh! Is he married?"

Is that the universally accepted reason for looking someone up on Facebook? To check their marital status?

"Funny you'd ask. I just clicked on another picture. I don't know, but there's a woman in the picture with him and a kid."

Lisette was oddly silent.

"Hello? Liz?"

"Yeah," she said somberly.

"What? Did you know about this?" I asked. "Is he married?"

"I'd heard he had a kid, but that's all," she said.

"And you didn't tell me?"

"Tell you for what?" Liz said, her voice a little louder. "Remember, I went through that breakup with you. It was excruciating, Jordan. So why would I ever bring him up again?"

I heard only part of what Liz was saying. "I could've handled it, you know."

"Jordie, you're not handling it now. I can hear it in your voice. Did you think he wouldn't move on? Honey, everybody moves on eventually."

"Humph, everybody but me, right?"

"That's not what I'm saying."

"That's probably his wife," I said, still only half listening.

"Maybe," she said.

"You would tell me, wouldn't you? You're not keeping it from me?"

"If I knew, yes, which I don't," Liz said. "But only because you asked. What does it say on his profile?"

"I don't know; I didn't look."

"You're a Facebook hater. Actually, I'm shocked you're on there at all. What made you join? I thought that wasn't your thing."

"I was doing some research for a story and got curious. Looks like he's still in Norfolk," I said. "There's nothing about his marital status, though."

"Well, he's probably not married, then, or maybe he doesn't share that publicly. You know how some guys are," Liz reasoned. "See there, if you'd married him, you'd be living in Norfolk, working in a smaller market and eating crab soup with dinner every other night."

Lisette was trying to cheer me up by mentioning a bad experience I'd had when I visited. Crab soup and shots apparently don't mix.

"Oh god!" I recoiled. "Why'd you have to bring that up?" Thinking back on the horror I felt in that moment, I was grateful that I could at least laugh about it now.

"Girl, it was so bad, you ruined crab soup for me," Liz said.

Finally I was listening.

"Thanks," I said. "I'll be okay. It was just a shock, you know? I thought I was over all that."

"It's understandable. But it doesn't mean you're not over him."

"Right."

My aunt told me once, "You never really fall out of love with someone; you just stop liking them. That's when you know it's over." But the albatross around my neck wasn't Lin; it was something even more intangible than an ex-fiancé with a baby and possibly a wife.

"Is it me, Liz?"

She feigned ignorance. "What do you mean? Is *what* you?"

"You know, like you said, everybody moves on. What have I moved on to? A career? Sure. Another city? But that doesn't change the fact that I haven't been in love or been loved by anyone since then."

A wound I thought had long closed opened and long-buried memories poured in.

"Hold on, Liz."

I grabbed my coat and purse and headed for the stairwell leading to the parking garage. Now I was alone but had placed myself in an echo chamber where my shaking voice and near tears would reverberate as effectively as if I were wearing a mic.

"Jordie? You there?"

"Yes, hold on. I'm going to my car."

"Your car?"

I bolted out the metal door to the garage. The building's warmth was quickly replaced with a biting cold that felt more like January than March weather. I got in my car and cranked up the heat.

"Okay, I'm back. Oh, Liz," I cried, "what's wrong me? Am I unlovable?"

"Don't be ridiculous. Of course you're lovable," she said. "You just haven't found *your* love yet."

"But I loved him, Liz! I loved him!" I pleaded. "Why did I give all that up?"

Lisette then asked the question I had been dreading since she told me about her engagement. "Jordan, is my getting married freaking you out?"

I hadn't thought of it that way, honestly, and was unsure how to respond. "I don't think so. No. I mean, I don't even have a date for the wedding."

"Do you need one?" she asked.

"I guess not."

I owed myself and Lisette a better explanation than fear over not having a wedding date for my meltdown. I knew that part of it was the feeling I got watching others' lives change around me while mine stayed the same. I detected a tinge of that sentiment today listening to Shelly Biltmore talk about her nephew and how he should have been her child. She wasn't envious of Marla, she felt abandoned by her. Shelly remained present but resented being pitied.

I don't want to end up like that.

"I think what I'm freaked out about is the fact that I don't know if I have it in me to be with one person," I said. "Marriage is surrender. I guess I'm just scared that I'll never be able to surrender myself like that to anyone, and I'll end up alone and miserable."

And there it was—the truth I had been reticent to admit.

"Sis, you listen to me and listen good."

Lisette always called me *sis* when she was about to say something serious.

"You had trepidations about marrying Lin and you didn't ignore them. That's a good thing! Look, I love Mike with my whole heart. There's not an iota of doubt in me that this man and I were meant to be together. You will find the one."

I laughed.

"You will," she insisted.

"Oh, I believe you," I said cynically. "No, I'm laughing because these talks, no matter how deep, always seem to end with 'Just hold on. The one is coming.'"

13

Friday, March 20

By Friday, I'd made up my mind to drive to Rensselaer, Indiana. When I woke up, I texted Shelly: Are you around today? Thinking about driving down there and having a look around.

OMG YES!! she wrote back.

Great. See you around 11:30.

I took the Chicago Skyway, an exotic name for a bland toll road that connects Chicago and northwestern Indiana. For miles, the scenery was a graveyard of abandoned mills. The exorbitant toll fees were well worth it if it meant fighting less traffic moving in and out of the city. I was in for a good three-hour drive round trip. Once I hit the toll road, the time passed quickly. Before long, I transitioned out of a midwestern city most people don't think of as the Midwest, where millions of people live in densely populated buildings, to the country, with acre upon acre of densely planted crops. The monotony of the landscape and the static from Chicago's top R&B station, whose frequency I'd lost miles ago, created an unqualified space for me to think about what Shelly had shared about her brother-in-law. Didn't Jim Hancock know that the husband was always a suspect? Was this guy really stupid enough to kill his wife during a divorce? With a potential custody trial? Knowing that his wife's next of kin despised him? She had been living in her hometown long enough for him to come to terms with the fact she wasn't coming back. Is that when he became a real threat? All I knew was, if this was his plan, he had to know it wouldn't work. Just ask the California husband who killed his pregnant wife.

Frankly, I was still in shock that Ellen, instead of emphatically stating, "No, drop it," basically gave me the go-ahead to chase my tail. By now Ellen should've known not to trust that I wouldn't. But technically I was playing offside again and could be reprimanded or worse. After all, over the years Ellen had often admonished me to stay in my lane and stick to my job, so of course I knew the deal. I decided to poke around in this town with fewer than six thousand residents who probably all knew one another, went to the same high school, and never left.

"Small town, big heart" professed the sign welcoming visitors to Rensselaer. I got there half an hour early. I had some time to kill and figured Main Street was a safe bet to take me into the heart of this small town. I passed a corner diner with its 1950s-era awning and signage. There was a billboard advertising a Classic Car Cruise Night held two weeks ago, and the Rensselaer police department headquarters were housed in a drab one-story building. Thus far all my expectations of a rural community had been met, but I was struck by the beauty of the town's courthouse. The Jasper County seat was a gothic structure built of Bedford limestone, with a clock tower rising out of the center, as regal as any landmark mansion in the English countryside. I expected to see more people milling around on a Friday and tried to spot some who looked like me.

Before I got in the car, I researched Rensselaer to see who lived there. Black and brown people made up less than five percent of the population of the county.

Shelly chose our meeting spot, a place where, if I was recognized, it wouldn't be a big deal.

"Shelly, can you promise me that you'll be discreet? I'm putting my job on the line here. Is there, like, a farmers' market or some other gathering spot in town that attracts tourists where we could meet?"

"Sure," Shelly said. "There's a flea market on the outskirts of town. I'll text you the address."

I anticipated an open-air market with tents and tables packed with farm-to-table-quality fruits and vegetables, homemade jams and soaps, and vendors selling arts and crafts, and other goods. For someone to drive an hour or more outside the city to go thrifting, antiquing, or to check out some fresh produce or handmade trinkets was not so unfathomable. But the Jasper Junction was altogether different, a flea market housed in a powder-blue low-rise building that sat along the road adjacent to a residential area.

I'm not going to blend in as much as I hoped.

Perfect timing—I grabbed a parking spot just as someone was pulling out. Inside, I was struck by the unmistakable flea market aroma of old, used things that was ever present. I did a quick scan of the room. Perhaps there were a few items worthy of the *Antiques Roadshow*, but mostly it was stuff people had held on to for far too long, and now they hoped or dreamed it was some secret treasure worth something.

"Jordan." The voice came from behind and I turned around to the startling image of Shelly Biltmore. That flaming red hair against her pale skin was her signature.

She leaned forward and whispered, "I don't know why we couldn't have just met at the farm. It's only about six or seven miles down the road."

Yeah, we're not there yet.

Call it a blessing, call it a curse, but I've grown an incredible intuition, an instinct about people. The minute I meet someone, my mind goes into investigation mode. At this point, it's like I can't help it. To be fair to Shelly, I didn't believe for a second she had anything to do with her sister's disappearance. I also didn't know if she hated her brother-in-law so much that she might be willing to blame him for something he didn't do.

"You kept your word. I'm surprised you came," she said.

"I told you I would, didn't I? Look, Shelly, if I'm going to do this, you've got to trust me."

One thing I've learned in life and in my line of work is that most people don't reveal the unfiltered, unfettered truth about themselves or someone they care about, especially something that could be perceived as negative. I'd listened to Shelly describe her sister in glowing terms, as I would my own sister. Whatever she was holding back, in a way I couldn't blame her. The media frequently practices victim blaming—highlighting one aspect of a person's character or an unflattering image or misstep to somehow explain how that individual ended up hurt or killed. Infuriating, but it happens.

"Okay," she said. "Follow me."

Shelly led me to the back of the store. That's when I first noticed the backpack she was carrying in her right hand, so heavy it practically dragged the ground.

"Where are we going?"

"To the back office," she said. "For privacy."

"Is it okay for us to just walk back there?"

"Yeah, don't worry. They know me here. I helped the owners set up their website a couple years ago. The internet connection is awful on the farm. When I need to, I come here and use theirs."

"Their website?" I asked.

"Long story," Shelly said.

Worried I'd break something, I followed her down a narrow aisle surrounded by rows of shelves crammed with various styles of glasses and dishes, something of a maze.

"Hey, Shelly!" A woman's voice blared behind us. I didn't want to turn for fear my huge purse might take out an entire shelf. Shelly waved but didn't turn around, clearly recognizing the voice. "Hi, Rose! I'll be in the back for a bit!"

"All right, then! Come by before you go!"

The windowless office was sparsely furnished. Shelly pulled her laptop from her bag and directed me to sit in a chair against the wall.

"I've had so much on my mind, Jordan, I forgot to ask: Did you ever see the screenshot I emailed to your newsroom? It was a conversation that Jim was having with someone online."

I had to think. "I don't remember that."

"Here. I'll show you."

She pulled up a file and turned the screen to face me so I could read it. The image had been magnified many times over, and the text was blurry but readable.

rubble&rock: She's not even a good mom.

Hapinfast: Well, isn't that the point of the divorce. To finally get rid of her?

rubble&rock: Only one way to be sure.

Hapinfast: What do you have in mind?

rubble&rock: I thought you wanted to play for keeps.

"Yes, I remember that now."

"Rubble&rock is the name Jim uses to stream a video game. I don't know who Hapinfast is. I figured out Marla's password. It wasn't hard. She uses the same password over and over, occasionally adding her kids' birthdays. I always warned her about that."

"What type of account is this?"

"It's a streaming site called Justin.tv. Marla doesn't play, really. She signed up more as a spectator."

I didn't know that watching other people play video games online was a thing. Shelly turned the laptop around and signed into Marla's account.

"Look," she said, pointing to a conversation.

Hapinfast: Are you doing alright?

MarleyGirl: No! I'm not! THIS CHEATING SOB IS THREATEN-ING TO TAKE MY KIDS!

Hapinfast: What are you going to do?

MarleyGirl: I need to get outta here.

Shelly shot me a look suggesting this dialogue that Jim wasn't part of somehow confirmed something about him.

"Marla is MarleyGirl. What the hell is this Hapinfast person doing talking to Jim about getting a divorce and buddying up to my sister at the same time?"

"Are there more chats between them?"

"Yeah."

Shelly continued to scroll down.

Hapinfast: I'm here for you whatever you need. How can I help?

MarleyGirl: OMG! You're so amazing! Call me—219-555-5210. Let's meet.

Hapinfast: OK, sounds good. It's about time.

"That was their last correspondence, which was over four months ago. But that doesn't mean they stopped talking. They just probably stopped talking on the site after Marla gave her her number. I'm assuming it's a woman."

It was dizzying. I hadn't played a video game since Tekken back in the mid-1990s, and that was only to bond with my younger cousins at the family reunion.

"I admit, I don't know anything about the gaming world. I didn't realize women were into it all that much. Certainly none of my friends are."

"Well, those that do, according to Marla, are stepping into a world with a lot of macho jerks," Shelly said. "Marla told me the men were immature and the women, based on some of the comments she read, were vulgar and desperate for attention. She said there was a lot more flirting and hooking up going on than actual competition. She just watches.

"I used to tease her and call her a virtual cheerleader to a bunch of men with arrested development," she continued. "She was just doing it because she was following Jim."

My mind was rushing to imagine this almost secret world. From my point of view, finding a release in the gaming world seemed fine. *Really, who cares? And isn't that safer than a lot of other addictions?*

"Couldn't she read his chat messages?"

I hoped I didn't sound totally ignorant, but for me, there was a learning curve.

"No. You can do a public or a private chat. The public chats disappear after a few hours. But you can read the private ones if you have someone's log-in," she said. "Check this out."

Shelly turned to the screen again and scrolled down a few pages. "See how far back this goes? Marla had been corresponding with this Hapinfast person for two months before the last message. Looks like they got pretty chummy."

"What's this here?" I pointed to a line on the screen. Shelly placed the cursor over a text from Hapinfast about a yoga club that meets on Saturdays.

"I think you're right about it being a woman."

"From Danville at that," Shelly said.

"Why are you showing me all this? Do you think it has something to do with Marla's disappearance?"

"I don't know. Not long after the date of this last message, I remember, things started happening fast."

"What things?"

"Marla was on a tear to get away from Jim. She bought a used Toyota RAV4, but she hid it from him. It's the car she drove here after she left him. When I asked how she got it, she avoided the question at first. But not long after, Marla opened up about just how bad things had gotten at home. That's when she confided she got the car from a friend and was paying for it in installments."

"She wasn't working. Where'd she get the money?"

"He did control the purse strings. The only direct access she had to money was paying the bills and taking care of the kids' things. She started taking out cash advances on the credit cards. And you know, that's not cheap. But Jim never noticed. I guess he didn't check the line items on the bill. She paid them all from the joint account, but he never stopped reminding her all the deposits were from him. She was banking on him never questioning the expenses. Oh, and then she told me about a diamond bracelet, a push present he gave her after their second child. She never liked it, though. Marla suspected Jim had been having an affair when she was pregnant. She never went into detail, but something went on. She sold it, and since she hardly wore it, she figured he wouldn't notice it was gone. She was happy to get rid of it. All it did was remind her of the affair."

"He admitted the affair?"

"I don't know much about it. I just know it happened."

So Marla wasn't just thinking about leaving; she'd been planning on leaving. What did that trigger in Jim? Is that what he meant by playing for keeps?

14

I didn't drive this far from home on my day off to spend it in a flea market. But I wasn't sure where to start. Was I supposed to call Jim Hancock and ask him about his missing wife? And if he had something to do with her disappearance, that wouldn't be the most pleasant introduction.

"Shelly, I really want to help you, but I don't have a lot to go on. The article I read about Marla's disappearance mentioned that she didn't show up for two appointments the day she went missing—a job interview and another to see an apartment."

"Yeah."

"Do you know where she was headed that day?"

"She was interviewing for a temp position at a tax office downtown. And she told me she was also going to check out some rental properties in Lafayette that would be big enough for her and the kids."

"Is Lafayette close?"

"It's about forty-five minutes away."

"Are you sure she never made it to Lafayette?"

"No. I mean yes, I checked. At least, she never arrived at the apartment complex she told me about."

Forty-five minutes. Something could have happened to Marla along the way. But since Shelly said she never made it there, what would be the point in going?

"Can you show me the tax office?"

"Sure."

"Great. I'll drive."

It took us less than five minutes to get downtown. I crept along just under the speed limit and tried to keep an eye out for security cameras that might have picked up Marla's car traveling in this direction. I spotted two on a bank building and another keeping watch over the grounds of a liquor store a block from the Jasper County courthouse. Even in a homespun community such as this, people weren't naive about the fact that bad things can happen. I already knew that getting a bank to give up security footage to a reporter would be nearly impossible. The liquor store? Maybe.

"When you reported Marla missing, did the police talk to anyone at the tax office?"

"They didn't have to. I called the day after Marla didn't pick up the kids and the manager said she was a no-show. Never called or nothing. I told that to the police when I reported her missing."

"Did the school call you when she didn't show up?"

"Yes. About an hour after she was due to pick them up. I was listed as their emergency contact."

"What did you think happened?"

"I figured she must've gotten held up in traffic coming back from Lafayette and her cell phone died or something."

Shelly bit into her bottom lip. "I called around, checked with friends. I even called Jim to see if he'd heard from her. Once it got dark, that's when I got scared. I knew something was wrong."

"Did the police check security cameras in the area to see if something could've happened to her before she went into the building?"

"I don't think so, because she never made it here. It was hard to get answers at first. The detective assigned to the case isn't a fan of mine. We've had some run-ins in the past."

I was curious what Shelly meant by *run-ins* but decided to let it go for now.

"A guy I went to high school with who works in the department told me they came by here, looked around a nearby park, went by her friend's house where she'd been staying. They even checked around the farm. But at the end of the day, other than her car, they didn't know what else to look for."

I pulled away from the front of the tax office and down a side street to access the parking lot around back, checking for cameras.

"Wait, you said they went by a friend's house where she'd been staying. You know, Shelly, I never asked, but I assumed that Marla was staying with you this whole time."

"She did for a while, yes."

"How long?"

"About a month before she moved in with Victoria, her best friend from high school. They'd lost touch but recently reconnected."

"So when she headed out the day she disappeared, it was from Victoria's house?"

Shelly reached down and started rifling through her backpack. Her body language made it clear to me that the question felt like a gut punch. "I think so. I can't imagine where else she'd be coming from."

I wasn't convinced that the downtown area was a dead end, but now I was intrigued and perplexed, frankly, by this new detail.

"Can you show me where Victoria lives?"

"Yeah, sure. Turn left out of the parking lot."

Why had Shelly let me believe all this time that Marla and the kids were staying with her?

After Shelly had shared such a painful recollection, I didn't want to be indelicate, but I couldn't help but feel I'd been misled.

"Shelly?"

"Yes?"

Out with it, Jordan.

"Were you and Marla estranged?"

"It's complicated."

"Okay, uncomplicate it for me."

"Make a right, then go straight," she directed.

There was silence as I followed Shelly's directive and slowly pulled out into the oncoming traffic.

"Shelly, did you hear me? Are you going to tell me what happened?"

Shelly drew in a long breath and let out a heavy sigh. "Moving back to Rensselaer was dreadful for Marla. That's why she was looking at Lafayette. It's pretty and it sits on a lake. She didn't want the kids to feel the shock of a new life; she could barely process it all," she said.

To end up right back where she started was a bridge too far for Marla Hancock. A side-by-side comparison of my life and Marla's was a stark juxtaposition. After graduating from college in Missouri, if I hadn't gone back to Texas close to where I started out, I wouldn't be where I am today.

"She was trying desperately to get a job, but obviously she needed Jim's support."

If Marla was cash-strapped, why didn't she just stay with Shelly? I pulled off to the side, parked, and shut off the car.

"What are you doing? What's wrong?" Shelly asked.

"Look, either tell me what's really going on or I'm taking you back to the flea market and going back to Chicago."

"What are you talking about, Jordan?"

"Why wouldn't she just temporarily stay with you? It doesn't make sense. You're holding back. I can't help you if you're not going to open up, Shelly."

She looked around as if she was debating bolting out of the car.

"*You* called *me*! We're in it now! I'm here, but you've got to take off the mask and trust me, already."

I'd tossed Shelly my best game pitch and she didn't even take a swing at it. *Does she think I'm bluffing?*

"Do something for me," I said.

"All right," she whispered. "If I can."

"Think back to when we first met. What was the one thing you wanted to tell me but were afraid to? I'm a vault. You can trust me, okay?"

She nodded.

"On the count of three, just blurt it out. Are you ready? One, two, three . . ."

"No, Jordan. You're just going to judge her like everybody else."

If you thought I would judge her, why did you come to me for help? By now I was exasperated but kept quiet. There was power in saying nothing.

Finally, barely audible, she spoke up. "You're right. We had a falling-out. But that's not what I've been afraid to tell you. Marla had been battling an addiction."

"Alcohol?"

"Yes, and prescription drugs. Antidepressants that her doctor had given her."

It was starting to make sense. Shelly wasn't being coy; she was fiercely protecting her sister's reputation.

"I told you she had the baby blues. Remember? The antidepressant helped at first, but after a while she was convinced it wasn't working, and she turned to alcohol. She started drinking more and more. She was a wreck and Jim wasn't there for her. He just made things worse. Instead of trying to get her help, he threatened to take the kids."

"So by the time she moved back here, was she still struggling with the addiction?"

"No, she'd spent a month in rehab. Can you imagine leaving your kids with someone you don't trust? She loved them enough to try and get herself together."

Kids rarely notice a mother's sacrifice, at least not until they're older. Everything from time to themselves, a pair of shoes, date night, or a trip they wanted to take took a back seat to their children's wants and needs and safety. I could only imagine what that felt like. The whole "mommy and daddy with 2.5 kids and a house in the suburbs" scenario was still not for me. I'd chosen a different path that required personal sacrifices. Any fallout, I owned it, but I was still deemed selfish for it by the men I'd dated. Coming from Lin, the word *selfish* grew spikes and cut deep. For months after, I replayed the scene of my ex-fiancé screaming at me across a table, my diamond engagement ring dislodged from my finger, twinkling like a lone star in the void between us.

At the risk of alienating Shelly, I pressed on. "What happened between you two?"

"Moving back home for Marla was a huge step. And I really thought this was it. I thought she was at peace with her marriage ending and was ready to move on. But a week before she went missing, I overheard her talking on the phone to that creep. I could hear only what she was saying, but she was going over apartment listings with him, and it sounded to me like she was still letting Jim make decisions for her."

"You confronted her?"

"Yes! I told her it wasn't up to him where she lived. She was acting like the old Marla, allowing herself to be controlled and in denial. She got mad at me for eavesdropping. I wasn't. I just happened to overhear her. And she accused me of pressuring her. She said she just needed time to figure things out."

"At any point did Jim try to persuade Marla to come back home?"

"No! He didn't fight for his family, but he knew she was going to need his help. Marla wasn't trying to break his bank account. But I told her she was crazy if she thought that cheap bastard was going to pay for her to live in some fancy lakeside townhouse."

The portrait of Jim Hancock that Shelly painted for me had two faces. He would threaten to take the kids one minute, but the next he was fine with his family splitting up if it didn't cost much to get Marla out of his hair. From what I'd witnessed of break-ups like this, most men, even those who had cheated, practically begged their wife to come home. Jim might have wanted to control Marla, but he didn't want her. He wanted his own life, too.

I still found it hard to believe that the sisters' argument escalated to the point where Marla would leave. So did Shelly.

"I think I hit a nerve when I told her that," Shelly went on, her voice beginning to crack. "I didn't expect her to just up and leave like that. I'm single, never married, no kids. Having her and the kids at the farm gave me . . . purpose. She said they all needed a break . . . from everybody."

"And that's when she left to go be with Victoria?" I asked.

"The very next day. And I haven't seen her since."

"So your sister was living right here in town and you two weren't in touch? How long ago was that?"

Shelly's tears flowed. I'd unintentionally ripped the bandage off a festering wound. It took her a moment to catch her breath.

"Almost two months ago now," she said, still struggling to breathe. "I called and called. I left messages, I sent her texts. Finally she wrote back that she needed space and she'd call me when she was ready."

Her shoulders shook, but there were no more tears. Shelly had been crying for so long now, I believe she was all cried out at last.

15

A reservoir of dark, murky water and two strategically placed brick pillars gave the impression of a grand entrance to Victoria's subdivision. While the area didn't qualify as a gated community, the homeowners association clearly wanted to signal some level of status. Welcome to the world of the aspirational middle class. It's not a bad place to be if you can reach it. The homes looked as if assembly-line workers had placed every brick and eave in mirror formation, with the goal of creating uniformity and a lack of individuality. This was exactly the kind of neighborhood where, if something terrible happened, reporters would recite the overused refrain "If it can happen here, it can happen anywhere." The coded language wasn't hard to decipher.

Shelly directed me to turn down the lone cul-de-sac in the subdivision. "It's right there in the middle," she said, pointing to a house that found a way to display an ever-so-slight glimpse of character, with patches of purple and white crocuses dotting the yard.

"Quaint," I said.

"You mean boring."

"No, I mean quaint," I said, Shelly's sharp view reminding me again of a resentment of a life she felt didn't welcome her, the outsider who was never let in.

Suddenly Shelly slid down in her seat, her shoulders gliding below the armrest so that her knees nearly touched the underside of the dashboard.

"What are you doing?"

"What if she sees me?"

"Are you serious?" I snapped.

Was Shelly truly afraid of being spotted? Her crouched posture reminded me of an undercover cop routine.

Is this what she thinks I do for a living? Lurking around, hiding in bushes, investigating leads?

To escape the absurdity of the moment, I probed Shelly further about Marla's relationship with Victoria. It must have hurt for her sister to run to someone else to be her comforter and best friend.

"Have you spoken to Victoria since Marla vanished?"

"Yes, of course we've spoken. But to be honest, she doesn't know any more than I do. She said she'd already gone to work by the time Marla headed out that day."

"So why are we here?"

"I wanted you to meet Victoria. Honestly, something feels off about her," Shelly said. "But I was afraid she'd shut me down if I called ahead and asked first. I figured we'd just drop by and see if she was at home."

That made no sense. When was showing up at someone's house unannounced ever a good thing? But by now I was too far in to turn back. I wanted to see if there was something to what Shelly's gut was telling her. I parked on the street in front of the house.

"We're going in?" Shelly asked.

I was no longer up for the challenge of concealing my annoyance. "We're here now. Let's at least see if she's home. Come on."

Just before we reached the landing, a woman opened the door. She was wearing black Victoria's Secret leggings that clung to her slender, muscular legs, a sign of a dedicated workout routine. Factor in the Chevy Suburban parked in the driveway and Victoria had everything Shelly led me to believe Marla wanted.

"Hey, Shelly? What's going on? I didn't know you were coming by."

"Hey, Vic, I'm sorry to drop in on you like this."

"It's all right. Have you spoken to Marla? Did she send you to get her things?"

Shelly looked as confused as I felt. "No." She frowned. "I want you to meet Jordan Manning. She's doing a story on Marla."

Victoria's disposition went from congenial to confrontational. "A story on Marla? What do you mean?"

I sensed the tension between these two women could escalate. I wanted to manage both their expectations before this exchange got out of hand. "I'm based in Chicago. I'm not even sure I'm doing a story. Shelly asked for my help. That's why I'm here."

Shelly's body language told me that wasn't what she wanted to hear from me. She wanted me to be fully committed, all in, but I wasn't there yet.

"She's been missing now for more than three weeks," I said.

"This has escalated to a missing person case?" Victoria asked.

"You seem surprised," I said. "What? You don't believe Marla's missing?"

"Wait a minute," said Shelly, exasperated. "Have you heard from her?"

Victoria shrugged her shoulders. "Well, no, I haven't. But that doesn't mean she's missing."

Is she really this naive?

Shelly said, "Can we go inside to talk about this?"

"Sure."

I trailed the two women as they walked side by side up the driveway, confused by Victoria's reaction and concerned that Shelly, who looked ready to explode, would unleash her pent-up frustration on Marla's friend the second we were behind closed doors.

Inside, Victoria led us past the foyer to a hall lined with a gallery of photographs that marked the passing of time. Baby and vacation shots, and boys posing with soccer balls and bats for their annual Pee Wee sports pictures. One image stood out.

"There she is," Shelly said, pointing to a picture of two women with wide smiles, arms looped around each other's waist and holding up the peace sign. A towering white cathedral provided one of the most beautiful backdrops in the South. They looked like they were having the time of their lives. It was the kind of picture that made you wish you were there.

"This was Marla and Victoria's trip to New Orleans," Shelly said.

"May I see?" Shelly handed me the picture, and nostalgia set in. "I thought I recognized the building. This is the St. Louis Cathedral in Jackson Square."

"Yep, sure is. Have you been there?" Victoria asked.

"Yeah. Once," I said.

Victoria managed an uneasy fake smile. Suddenly two little boys who looked to be around six or seven sped past us in a blur through the dining room.

"That's my son Jeremy and his friend. My daughter's at day camp. Jeremy had the sniffles this morning, so I kept him home.

As you can see, he's gotten over whatever it was. Boys, stay out of the fridge!"

"You know what, Vic?" Shelly interjected. "Now that you mention it, I should pack up some of Marla's things while I'm here. Can we go back to her room?"

Can we go back to why Victoria is acting like she's surprised Marla's missing?

"I think we should leave her things alone until she gets back," Victoria said. "You know Marla's sensitive about her stuff."

I couldn't let it slide a second time, and neither could Shelly. "So you don't believe Marla's missing?" I asked. "How can you be so sure she's coming back? Do you think Marla doesn't want to be found? And why would she leave all her things behind?"

"Yeah, what the hell do you think she's doing, then?" Shelly asked.

"Why are you attacking me? I haven't done anything wrong!"

"Because you seem to know more than you're letting on!" Shelly said, inching closer to confront Victoria. This situation was threatening to come to a head. "If you know something, you need to tell us what it is! Now!"

Shelly's odd behavior in the car was starting to make sense. I gathered that these two women didn't care for each other, which was the reason this situation had escalated so quickly—I hoped not to the point that Victoria would ask us to leave. Shelly had assumed her role in this "good cop, bad cop" scenario. Now it was my turn.

"Ladies, I know this is a stressful time for both of you," I said. "Victoria, I appreciate you letting us pop in like this. I want to hear what you have to say."

Victoria cupped her hand around the back of her head to manage the stress that likely was gathering. "I think Marla needed a break. A lot has happened, you know. Once she has time to reset, I think she'll come back and figure things out," she said.

"Ex*cuse* me!" Shelly yelled. "Since when have you known her to take a break from her children? And in the middle of a custody battle? Are you insane?"

Marla had taken a break before to go to rehab. But bringing that up now wasn't going to help the situation.

"Shelly," I said, "let's take a moment, okay? Victoria, if I thought Marla had gone off to take some time for herself, I wouldn't be here. Look, you're her best friend. There are things I tell my best friend I wouldn't even share with my sister. But please, be honest. Have you heard from Marla? Do you know where she is?"

"No! I don't know where she is!" Victoria tossed back, directing her ire at Shelly.

"Okay, okay, everybody calm down. Let's go check out Marla's room. Shall we?" I asked.

I tapped the back of Shelly's hand and gave her a pointed glance I hoped she would correctly interpret as "I've got your back."

Marla's room was in the far corner of the house next to the laundry room.

"Here it is. I haven't moved anything," Victoria said.

"Really?" I asked. "You haven't touched anything in here?"

Victoria shook her head.

"Has anyone? The police?" I asked.

"Just Jim. But he only took the kids' stuff."

"Marla and the kids all stayed in this room together?" I asked.

"Yes. That couch lets out into a bed. Marla slept there. She let the kids have the bed."

I wondered what it must have been like for Marla to flee a cheating, emotionally and perhaps even physically abusive husband, leaving behind the world she'd so carefully created for herself only to end up hunkered down with two small children inside her best friend's perfect slice of suburbia. Would that be enough of a life setback to make a mother leave her children? From what I had learned of Marla, that would be a hard no. Was she regretting the choices she'd made? Did seeing how things turned out for Victoria in their native Rensselaer make Marla wish she'd married a local guy and raised her kids close to her family, instead of ending up with a far-from-perfect man in a state where she had no family or friends?

"Is everything in here Marla's, or do you have some of your stuff in here, too?" asked a calmer Shelly.

"I cleaned out the room for her. Everything in here is hers except for a couple of blankets and a bathrobe she borrowed."

Shelly pulled open the top two dresser drawers and started grabbing clothes by the armful and spreading them out on the bed. "Jordan, do me a favor and hand me that suitcase."

"I'll get a couple of boxes from the garage," Victoria said.

For a moment, I almost followed Shelly to help, caught up in the swirl of everything happening. Then I came to my senses. I was a reporter, not a family member or a friend. When I left home this morning, no way would I have guessed I'd be rummaging through Marla's belongings. This had officially gotten weird. I didn't know Victoria. She made me uncomfortable. The police hadn't even dusted for prints in here, and the last thing I wanted was my fingerprints all over this room. As far as I was concerned, it was a crime scene.

"Hold on, Shelly. Let's think about this before we start touching things. There could be something here that could give us an idea of what happened to Marla, and we don't want to contaminate any potential evidence."

"Like what?" Shelly asked. "Her clothes? Jewelry?"

Victoria returned with two midsize boxes with lids. "Do you have any rubber gloves? Oh, and some ziplock bags, too?"

"Sure."

"Brand new?"

"No problem. I'll be right back."

"Thanks."

Despite my warning, Shelly started shoving Marla's clothes into one of the boxes. Not in the delicate manner one would expect someone to handle the personal effects of a departed loved one, but more as if she was angry, imagining herself chastising her sister for causing all this drama, thinking, *When she finally shows back up, I'm going to let her have it.* I'd seen this before when someone goes missing. Family members have two possibilities in mind. One, the reunion, and the other—well, we all know the other.

"Shelly, wait until Victoria gets back with the gloves. We don't know who all's been in this room. She already told us Jim was in here."

I glanced around, taking in every detail of the room. By the time I turned to face Shelly again, she was consumed by grief. Tears flooded her face.

"I know this can't be easy for you, but we're here now. I just want to be sure we do things right, okay?"

Victoria bounced back into the room, almost out of breath. "Sorry. It took me forever to find them," she said. "I have no idea how I even remembered they were under the sink."

I instructed both Victoria and Shelly to put the gloves on. Shelly's eyes and nose, even her ears, glowed red. She was full of pain, but Victoria didn't show Shelly an ounce of compassion. *Does she not see how upset she is?*

"Did Marla carry more than one purse?" I asked.

"Sure. Don't we all," Victoria said.

"Do you know where she kept them?"

"They should be on a hook in the closet."

Victoria slid open the mirrored double doors. The closet was jam-packed with clothes, a denim jacket, a thick cardigan, a couple of sweatshirts, a weekender tote bag with Marla's initials on it, a pair of sneakers, a couple of pairs of jeans weighing down one hanger, and a few sweaters.

"Here they are," Victoria said, presenting two small nylon handbags with long straps and the tote.

"Is there anything in them?"

"I don't know. Like I said, I haven't gone through her stuff," she said.

Shelly mentioned earlier that Victoria and Marla had lost touch but recently reconnected. Victoria seemed sympathetic toward Jim. Could she be the woman Marla was conversing with in the gaming chat room?

"Okay, grab a clean sheet and spread it over the bed, and dump out all the contents."

I hovered over Victoria and Shelly as they picked through the contents. A pack of gum, a tube of lip balm, one silver earring, and a travel-size package of Advil.

"These are the only two bags I've ever seen her carry," Victoria said. Then simultaneously, Shelly and I both looked at Victoria and asked, "Where's her wallet?"

"I guess she took it with her," Victoria answered.

"But why would she take her wallet and leave her purse?" Shelly asked.

"I-I-I don't know." Victoria shrugged. "She must've been carrying a different purse that day. It's not like I took inventory of her things, you know."

"Last I saw her, she was carrying the wallet I sent her for Christmas last year. It's the type you can attach your keys to. She kept her credit card and her ID and the kids' health insurance cards in there," Shelly said.

"Do you have any of Marla's laundry?" I asked.

"No. I washed all hers and the kids' things before Jim came to pick the kids' stuff up."

Didn't she say she hadn't touched anything in here?

"He waited for me to do the laundry. I told him Marla would kill me if I let them leave without clean clothes. So I did a fifteen-minute fast wash, and he waited around."

"What did he have to say?" I asked.

"He talked about how much his family means to him. The kids and Marla."

Shelly rolled her eyes.

"He said he wanted to go to marriage counseling. He's provided a pretty good life so she could stay home with the kids. Who wouldn't want that? That's exactly what I have here. I mean, Greg, that's my husband, he's always told me, 'Look, if you want a career, I have no issue with that.'"

Shelly managed to slip in a dig. "Oh, we see who's president of the Jim Hancock Fan Club."

Who knew that would be Victoria's breaking point? "You know what, Shelly? I'm sorry that finding a good husband didn't work out for you. But everybody doesn't want to be miserable and alone."

"Shut up, Victoria!"

Victoria ripped off the kitchen gloves. "I think you both

should leave. And why do I need these stupid gloves, anyway? This isn't a crime scene. Shelly, you can take the rest of Marla's things. Fine. That's between you and her. I just know that as soon as she shows back up, I'm going to tell her everything that happened here."

What just happened?

"Victoria, wait, wait, wait. Okay? I'm sorry. I didn't mean to upset you. I understand this is your best friend. You love each other. None of us know what happened here. Just please, give us a few more minutes to look around, and then we'll get out of your hair."

Shelly shook her head. I knew it couldn't have been easy.

"Fine," said Victoria, throwing up her hands.

"If you're not going to wear gloves . . ." I started to say.

"Don't worry. I'm not going to touch anything."

Shelly resumed rummaging through Marla's jacket pockets and pulled out a handful of tissues, a receipt from a restaurant called Mary's Diner, and an auto dealership business card. "'Rhodes Auto Dealers. Ronald Bridgeforth, sales associate,'" Shelly read out loud, shrugging her shoulders.

"Turn it over. There's something written on the back," I said.

She turned the card around. "Looks like it says Sa . . . vannah? And there's an address."

"Let me see," I said.

"It's Marla's handwriting," Shelly said, then faced Victoria, who was still sulking in the corner.

"Hmm. Vic, you ever heard of a Savannah?"

16

Shelly told Victoria she would come back in her truck to retrieve Marla's belongings. Our ill-planned visit left us both with more questions than answers. Before we left, something surprising happened. "Mind if I have a word with you?" Victoria asked me.

"Um, sure," I said, confused.

Shelly was visibly irked but didn't protest. "Fine, I'll meet you at the car."

Victoria waited until Shelly was far enough away to move in closer. "Listen, the last thing I wanted was to get caught in the middle of all this. Jim's a good guy, okay? I know Shelly hates him, but she hates everybody except her sister and those kids. But Marla and I have been best friends since the third grade, and I know Shelly. Don't let her take you on some scavenger hunt to nowhere. I don't know where Marla is. I truly don't. I just know that she's okay and she's going to call. I just know it."

Was she in denial? Was it too painful to admit something was wrong? Or was it just easier to pretend nothing had happened? Why was she siding with Jim over Shelly? Did she not know about his berating Marla about the baby weight? Had Marla not shared these stories with her best friend? Was Shelly exaggerating?

"You haven't talked to her?"

"I promise, I haven't."

Nothing Victoria said added up. Didn't Marla realize that abandoning her children like this would damage her custody case? Maybe Marla and Jim couldn't make it because they both were extreme contradictions. Jekyll and Hydes.

"If you're so confident she's coming back, will you call me when you do hear from her?"

Victoria took a long pause before answering, her jowls tightening. She looked almost defiant. "I'll leave that up to Marla."

"All right. Here's my card."

Victoria's behavior was more than peculiar; it was suspicious.

Shelly was leaned up against my car with her arms folded, pouting.

"What'd she say to you?" Shelly asked.

"She was embarrassed about her outburst, and she apologized," I said, walking around to the driver's side. Shelly looked at me as though she knew I was lying but moved on.

I pulled away from the curb, not sure where we were headed next.

"What's your relationship with Victoria?"

"I've known her practically my whole life. She's always been a little quirky, but . . ." She trailed off.

"I have to say this, Shelly, and don't get angry, but she paints an entirely different picture of Marla and Jim than you do."

"Okay, so just like Marla, everything Victoria says is right, huh? She can do no wrong?"

"Shelly, apparently there's a lot of history here that I'm not trying to get in the middle of. I'm just trying to figure things out and stay focused here. Do I think Marla left town of her own free will without any clothes? No, I don't. And you're right about the handbag. Why would she take only her wallet? Look at what was left in the closet. I assume she left with the clothes on her back. But why? If she had planned to go away, she sure didn't take much with her."

"Right. What you saw in that closet was what she left the farm with."

I didn't want to hurt her, but I had to ask. I probably already knew the answer.

"I know you said Marla and Victoria reconnected recently. But I get the feeling, based on everything that's happened today, that Marla and Victoria were closer than the two of you. Maybe she's right and Marla's not missing or in any danger."

Maybe I'm wasting my time here.

Shelly was about to answer but then stopped short. "Jordan, she's my sister. They do have more in common, sure, them both being moms and wives and all. But she's my sister, and I know she wouldn't walk away from those kids."

I wanted to tell Shelly, "That matters to you, but the circumstances don't care." There are a lot of people who go missing who don't want to be found. It happens. A mother's love is amazing, but the notion that mothers don't just up and leave is a fallacy. Mothers can reach their breaking point, too. Was Marla one of those people?

"I'm curious. What did Victoria say when the story ran in the Indy paper?" I asked.

"When I told her about it, she was frustrated with me for talking to the reporter at the *Rensselaer Republican.* That was her story that got picked up in the Indianapolis paper," she added. "The reporter is still interested. It's not a dead story to her."

That was the same article Ellen tracked down on the news portal.

"Think, Shelly. Are you sure she never mentioned the name Savannah?"

"I don't ever remember her mentioning a Savannah. Maybe she works at the dealership. Her name was on the back of the card."

"Right. Not just her name but also an address. You sure she didn't buy the car from a dealer? And if so, how'd she get credit approval without a job?"

"All I know is, Marla told me a friend helped her get the car. But she never told me the friend's name. So we've got nothing." Exasperated, Shelly struck the passenger window with the side of her fist.

"Don't give up," I said. "I'll check with the dealership. Okay?"

She closed her eyes and rubbed her forehead. Spending the day with Shelly revealed her to be equal parts detailed and disorganized. Loyal to a fault, but also a loose cannon who was willing to show up unannounced at someone's house, reporter in tow.

"Okay."

It was approaching three o'clock, closing time at the Jasper Junction. My mind went back to Victoria and the article about Marla's disappearance in the Indianapolis paper. As I pulled up next to Shelly's dark blue Chevy pickup, I had to ask. "Did Victoria even read the article?"

"Probably not. Vic is so deep into being the perfect mom, she never thinks of anything or anyone beyond her husband and her kids. I think she enjoyed having Marla's kids around, with them being so close in age to her kids and all. Their lives practically mirrored one another."

Shelly tried hard to mask her resentment, but I read between the lines.

"Who's the reporter at the local paper you spoke to?"

"Her name's Mimi Maxwell. I last spoke with her a couple of days ago. But she promised me a follow-up call. She seemed sincere when she said it."

"Do you have her number?"

"Yeah, I have her card in my truck. I'll grab it."

I hoped it wouldn't be much longer. It was time for me to go home. I kept the car running while Shelly grabbed the card from her truck. "Here, take this one. I've got another."

"Thanks."

"I know you have to go. I put you through a lot today. Thank you . . . for coming."

"It's all right," I said.

"Jordan?"

"Yes?"

"Do you believe she's dead?"

Do I believe it? Yes, but I have no proof and it would be irresponsible of me to say so.

"No. I mean, I don't know."

Within seconds, I worked through my disbelief about who to trust and found my allegiance. "I believe you, Shelly. I'm not going to let this go."

The look on her face told me she'd been waiting to hear someone say that to her for a very long time. Maybe her entire life.

"Thank you, Jordan. So now what?" she asked.

I grabbed the reporter's notebook I kept stuffed in the car door's side panel and a pen and handed it to Shelly. "Here," I said, "write down Jim's number."

Shelly took the pen and pad but stopped short of putting pen to paper. She looked up at me. "You're going to call him, right?"

"I think I have to, don't you?"

She nodded and jotted down the number.

"Oh, and one more thing," I said. "What's the detective's name you spoke to at the sheriff's department?"

"Flanagan. Lieutenant Bob Flanagan."

"Okay, thanks. I don't have to tell you to keep your phone close. I promise, I'll be in touch."

17

Shelly pulled out of the parking lot, her tires kicking up the dusty gray gravel as she sped out onto the lonesome rural highway. I, on the other hand, would not be so lucky. To leave Rensselaer at this time on a Friday meant hitting the now-inescapable traffic strangling Chicago's freeways. No commuters or basketball fans headed north to watch the Bulls play at the United Center to blame. Just a break in the wintry weather drawing people to the city in pursuit of a life in sharp contrast to what I had just witnessed at Victoria's.

I had been off the grid for more than five hours, and by now the only thing more clogged than the Dan Ryan Expressway was my voicemail. One message in particular came as a shock.

"Hey, Jordan. It's Nate. Are we still on for tonight? I have to be up early. But I'm free around six-thirty or seven if you're still up for drinks. Let me know."

Damn, that was two hours ago. He might have made other plans by now. *Don't overthink it, Jordan. Just text him back.*

Got your message. Driving back from Indiana. 7 is good. Pick a spot. See you soon.

Mimi Maxwell was my next call. But I wanted to look up Mimi's latest coverage first. I tapped into the flea market's Wi-Fi signal and found a longer version of the AP story on the *Rensselaer Republican*'s website.

Mother of 2, Native of Rensselaer, Reported Missing

Feb. 27, 2009

By Mimi Maxwell
Staff writer

The family of a 35-year-old mother of two from Danville, Kentucky, who had recently moved back to her native Rensselaer, Indiana, has reported her missing. Marla Hancock was last seen dropping off her 4-year-old daughter at a day care on East Angelica Street. Relatives say it's been four days and no one has heard from her.

According to her sister, Shelly Biltmore, who lives in Rensselaer, Marla didn't show up on Monday for a job interview. She also missed a scheduled visit to see an apartment, Biltmore said.

She was last seen driving a 2002 blue Toyota RAV4 with Kentucky license plate number AEO795.

Anyone who has information is asked to call 219-555-4444.

A young mother of two in the middle of a contentious divorce, attempting but on track to rebuild her life, had vanished. The mishandling of this investigation by local authorities was troubling, downright suspect, and it was time someone called them on it. I'd tried to keep an open mind without ignoring my suspicions, but nothing Shelly had described to me about Marla would suggest she just cut and ran. What was Victoria even talking about? And how could police be satisfied that Marla split of her own will because her credit card was used in Chicago? Not only was it professional malfeasance, but that narrative would be damaging to Marla's character if it got out. It made sense now why Shelly saw me as a last resort.

I hoped Mimi Maxwell could shed some light on this. En route to the interstate highway, I dialed the number on the business card.

Mimi answered on the first ring. "Hello. Mimi speaking."

Impressive. In response to an unknown caller at that. That's a reporter for you. "Hi, Mimi. This is Jordan Manning from News Channel 8 in Chicago. Got a minute?"

"Uh, sure. What can I do for you?"

"I'm looking into a missing person case. Marla Hancock? You wrote about it."

"Yeah."

"I'm just wondering what's going on with local law enforcement. I was in Rensselaer today with her sister, Shelly. Police hadn't even checked out her friend's house where Marla was staying."

"Oh, believe me. I'm frustrated, too. I've been calling, but they seem determined to believe that she just got up and vanished. It's a weakness of some police officers, I think. Once they are convinced of a version of what happened, it's hard for them to let go."

Amen to that, sister.

"Shelly told me that the police said Marla's debit card was used at an ATM in Chicago," she went on. "She must have opened her own account, because she told me Jim cut off her access to all his credit. Local police won't go on the record, and the public information officer for Chicago PD never called me back."

"Linda Folson."

"Yes, that's the one. I must've left a half-dozen messages."

"Trust me, Linda hasn't leaked a tip to the press a day in her life. She's a fortress. She's not going to say a word until her boss gives her the go-ahead. Are you still following the story?"

"I am, but I've been assigned something else and am trying to do both. But I have to tell you, your timing could not have been better."

"How so?"

"I just learned something that might convince my editor to put me back on the story. This is off the record," she said, stressing each syllable. "I have your word?"

"Yes. You can trust me. I'm a vault."

"Let me call you right back," she said abruptly.

I took the next exit and pulled into a gas station, filled up, and was back on the road and ready to give up on Mimi Maxwell's returning my call when my phone rang.

"Hello, Mimi?"

"Yes."

"Hi. I was worried you weren't going to call back."

"Well, to be honest, I did a little research of my own. I thought your name sounded familiar, and then I remembered a friend of mine interned in Chicago a couple years ago and she had mentioned you."

"So you were looking me up?"

"Absolutely," she said, unapologetic. "I was about to launch right in, but I needed to make sure of who you were, so I looked you up online. You can probably tell I'm very passionate about this story."

"Good. So am I."

I couldn't ignore the symmetry of our paths. The journalist in me wanted an explanation. But my nerd brain, as Liz called it, the forensic science side, found it reasonable to hypothesize that Marla ran from the life she thought she always wanted and was now in hiding.

"A source at the sheriff's department told me they're waiting on a key piece of evidence."

"The Cook County sheriff?"

"No, a Jasper County sheriff's deputy told me that in strict confidence. Denise . . . I mean, the sheriff's deputy told me that's why the police haven't said anything."

If the card was used at a bank ATM, that could mean only one thing.

"They have video."

"She didn't say for sure."

"But that was days ago. What's taking so long?"

"Good question. The only thing I can think of is the bureaucracy. Now we're talking about an investigation across two states, which means the Indiana and Illinois state police could already be involved."

She was probably right. I'd seen this happen before when multiple departments get pulled into an investigation and end up arguing over jurisdiction and ownership of the evidence. If Mimi was correct, then this story was about to go from below the radar to a national lead.

"Are you planning to write anything anytime soon?"

"My editor's got me on a short leash, but yes, as soon as I can get a comment on the record."

I was surprised by the way Mimi opened up so willingly about what she'd learned. But people outside the business have no idea that when a reporter fights for but still doesn't get support from the people steering the mother ship, they can feel a sense of helplessness. When those feelings aren't rectified, it can mean all bets are off. I was going to use it to my advantage.

"By the way, Mimi, I'll share with you that Shelly and I went to pick up some of Marla's things at her best friend's today and . . . Sorry, can you hold on? I've got another call coming in."

It was Shelly.

"I've got to take this. Let's stay in touch, okay?"

"Will do and thanks for the heads-up."

I clicked over to find Shelly crying hysterically.

"Shelly, what's wrong?"

"It's not her!" she cried.

Did the police find a body?

"Shelly, calm down. I don't understand. What do you mean, it's not her?"

"Okay, I'm trying," she said, struggling to breathe.

"Right after I left you, the sheriff's office called. They asked me to come in and look at some footage they got from an ATM camera in Chicago. The one where Marla's card popped up."

"Really? And you're saying it wasn't Marla on the tape?"

"No!" she cried.

"Was it a woman?"

"Yes, it was a woman. Jordan, she was wearing Marla's winter jacket with the hood pulled over her head."

"Could you see her face?"

"No, I couldn't make it out. But no way that was Marla. This person was taller and a lot thinner."

"You could tell that even through the jacket?"

"I could see her hands. She had slender fingers, and she wasn't wearing any jewelry. Marla wore rings on both her hands, including a birthstone ring she never took off."

Now, this changes everything.

"Oh my god, Jordan! She's dead, isn't she? My sister's dead!"

I had been on the highway for more than a half hour already. It was too late to turn back now.

"Shelly, listen to me. Try and calm down," I said. "Let's not jump to any conclusions, okay?"

"Somebody abducted her! I knew it! I knew she wouldn't just take off!"

Shelly's venting continued, and I couldn't blame her. This development was not a hopeful sign that Marla was still breathing. Someone had possession of her wallet and was wearing her coat. If this person had been nothing more than a thief, they wouldn't have gone to the trouble of trying to hide their face from the cameras at the bank. Were they trying to throw police off track? Then it occurred to me: *Did Marla herself orchestrate the whole thing?*

"Are you still at the police station?"

"Yeah, I ran out to my truck. I'm just sitting in the lot. I can't move, Jordan. I can't move!"

"Shelly, I need you to move, okay? Stay on the line with me, but go back in there. I want to talk to this Lieutenant Flanagan."

18

I could have just called the sheriff's department myself but wasn't up to getting the runaround. Surely this lieutenant who had just witnessed Shelly's reaction to this startling development would not shun her moments after dealing such a heavy blow.

"What do you want me to do?" she asked.

"Get to Flanagan and hand him your phone. I want to speak with him myself."

"Okay, I'm walking back in now."

The Jasper County sheriff's office was devoid of the bustling sounds of multiple phones ringing and the dissonance of voices on top of voices that I was accustomed to hearing at a Chicago police precinct. It was as quiet as a hospital.

"Good. He's right where I left him," Shelly whispered. "Excuse me, Lieutenant. I have someone who would like to speak with you."

"Oh? Who, may I ask?"

"Here. I'll let her tell you herself."

"Hello?"

"Lieutenant Flanagan? This is Jordan Manning with News Channel 8 Chicago."

For the second time today, Shelly had ambushed someone

with a news reporter. He must have looked apprehensive or worse, ticked off.

"Talk to her!" I heard Shelly order him. "She's trying to help."

After a brief pause, Flanagan finally spoke. "Hello, Miss Manning. I hope you know that I cannot comment on an ongoing investigation."

"Lieutenant, please, if you would, just listen for a moment. Shelly has confirmed that the woman in that video at the bank ATM is not her sister. She's a reliable source, so I will be reporting this. Now, what I need to know from you is whether this changes how you're going to conduct this investigation moving forward?"

"Beg pardon. What do you mean?"

"Well, up until now, I wasn't sure if you were even viewing this as a missing person case. Marla Hancock vanished over three weeks ago. Yet her best friend seems to think she just skipped out on her kids to take some time off for self-awareness. I know it must be confusing," I said, giving him some grace for inconsistencies that also had me scratching my head.

"Are you now ready to say that this is indeed a missing person case and that it is highly likely that Marla was taken against her will and could now be in imminent danger, or worse?"

"Miss Manning, I'm not sure what you're accusing me of, but at no time did I ever tell Miss Biltmore that we weren't viewing this as a missing person case."

"Then, why'd she have to go all the way to Chicago to find me to get someone to take this case seriously?"

"Is that what she told you? We're not taking this case seriously?"

"Forget it! Give me back my phone," I heard Shelly say in the background.

"You wanted me to talk to this lady. I'm talking to her," he said defiantly.

"Give it back!"

"Miss Biltmore!"

What the heck is going on?

"Lieutenant? Hello?"

I could hear Shelly going off in the background then suddenly her voice was muted.

"Pardon me, Miss Manning, but your buddy here just lost it. I asked one of my female officers to escort her to the back. If she keeps it up, I will have her arrested."

"What?"

"Actually, I'm glad we're talking because there's a lot you don't know. A lot she apparently doesn't want you to know."

"Like what?"

"Forty-eight hours after Marla Hancock was reported missing, a video camera located outside a retail store in downtown Rensselaer captured Marla getting in and out of her car."

"Where downtown?"

"Outside Montesi's Liquors."

Damn it! I knew I should have gone in there and asked about the video, but I got distracted by Shelly's omission that Marla was actually living with Victoria when she went missing.

"And Shelly knew about this?"

"Yes, but she wanted to believe her sister's husband had harmed her and nothing I could say could convince her otherwise."

"Did you talk to her husband?"

"I did, and his alibi is airtight."

"How can you be so sure? Shelly told me that Jim showed up in Rensselaer the day after she went missing to pick up their kids. He could've been there already."

"Look, we reached out to him, and he said he was attending a banquet in Danville the day Marla was last seen. It checked out. He offered to come in and we told him there was no reason to."

Why had Shelly kept this from me?

"At the time, there was more evidence pointing to her taking off than someone making her disappear," he said. "But even before the ATM video, we hadn't ruled out foul play."

"And you are aware she and her husband are estranged?"

"Yes, her sister made that quite clear."

Things were beginning to come into focus. After Jim's whereabouts were confirmed by police and Marla was captured on video, then Shelly likely came across to the police as nothing more than a bitter in-law.

"I spoke to her husband a few times, in fact. Sounds like the poor guy did all he could to make his marriage work. Trust me, I get it."

The hell? Is this guy relating his own internalized bias to explain what happened here?

"You said you looked at the video from the liquor store. I counted at least five other cameras within that block. You only got video from one of them?"

"Miss Manning, it was her," he said, avoiding the question.

"Did the liquor store video show Marla's face?" I pressed on. "If you didn't see her face, then how can you be sure it was her? Apparently, the bank video in Chicago didn't turn out to be her."

"And again, that's according to her sister! Look, I can't tell you who to believe or who not to believe. But I wouldn't go on air with any of this until we can be a hundred percent for certain that Shelly Biltmore isn't leading us on a wild-goose chase in an attempt to frame her brother-in-law."

"One more question, Lieutenant. Did Shelly see the liquor store video?"

"No," he said.

"Why not? Do you think she's lying about the bank video not being her sister?"

"I've answered your questions. Good day, Miss Manning."

"What's going to happen to Shelly?" I started to ask, but he was gone.

19

I was making good time before traffic slowed to a crawl at the fork dividing the interstate and the toll road. The day was a blur but even more than that, there was a refrain playing over in my head like a skipped record. *You got played.* The police seemingly had no confidence in Shelly, and now neither did I. Did she hate Jim enough to ignore all the signs? Or did she love her sister so much she could believe only the best about her?

Darkness brought the day to an end but there was still time to salvage the night. I was about to give up on hearing from Nate when he texted, **How's Pops for Champagne?**

Excellent choice. Pops was one of my all-time favorites. It could be romantic under the right circumstances but still cool for girls' night out, which was perfect, given I didn't know what I was getting into or which Nate would show up—the one who pouted because he felt I was ignoring him or the charming, confident man who winked at me in the checkout line during a late-night junk-food run to the Jewel-Osco.

I regretted not pushing back the date until seven-thirty; by the time I got home, it was clear I wouldn't be on time.

Sorry, Nate, I'm running a few minutes behind. See you soon, I wrote.

His reply read slightly if not fully annoyed. **Not surprised, but okay.**

Nate Fisher didn't know me well enough to not be surprised. He probably thought I had been rummaging through
my closet looking for the perfect outfit. He had no idea why I
was running late, and I didn't plan on telling him. Tonight I
wouldn't talk about work and risk driving a wedge between
the med student studying to save lives and me, the reporter
searching for someone whose life might have already ended.
Nate could think of our career objectives as similar in mission
and purpose. He could admire my gumption, lean in and hang
on every word, seem genuinely interested by asking questions
and nodding his head. But I wouldn't test that hypothetical tonight. I'd been slow to learn how to tiptoe around men's inse-
curities. Lieutenant Commander Lin Jackson was in my head
again. Why, after the talk I'd had with Lisette, was he back? I
thought I'd exhausted all thoughts of him, like the mixtape I
played so much in high school it started skipping and I stopped
listening to it. Then one day, inexplicably, I popped it into the
tape recorder, and it played straight through without missing
a beat. That was past-tense Lin in the present tense. And I had
this poor missing mom, who fell through the trapdoor I leapt
over, to thank for it.

I eased the soft, blush-toned cashmere sweater carefully over
my head, with a shift to the right to expose my shoulder, setting up the exact vibe I wanted to give tonight. The taxi let me
off directly in front of Pops. From this vantage point, I could
see through the floor-to-ceiling windows that the place was
packed, but no Nate. It looked no different from the inside. I
scanned the room searching for him. Then there he was, sitting at a high table by the window, all smiles, chatting up a
woman who was cracking up laughing. Her exaggerated posture was performative. She leaned in inches away from his face,

elbows propping her up, hands under her chin and back arched to accentuate her butt.

What did I just walk in on?

I don't remember Nate being that funny. But he sure had her howling. Nate had now turned into Bernie Mac. Who knew? Nate was handsome, no doubt, but more unassumingly so. He wasn't the first guy you spotted, but I understood how he could become the one you remembered. Now seeing a woman pay him all this attention irked me and aroused my competitiveness.

Nate's back was to the door when I walked in, and he seemed startled when I pressed my hand softly into it.

"Hi there," I said. "What's going on?"

"Oh, hi. You're here."

Nate stood and gave me a warm friendly hug, but instead of playing it the same way, I seized the moment, holding on to my prize and leaning back, my gaze trained on him. "Hi-i-i."

"Jordan, this is Jonie."

"Oh? You two know each other?"

"Well, not really—we just met," she said, still performing her sultry but coy mating routine.

Does she think we are cousins?

"Ah. I guess I assumed since you knew her name."

"Are you okay?" he asked.

"Yeah. I'm great!"

I noticed a mixed bouquet of roses, daisies, and irises lying across the opposite seat. The unmistakable convenience or grocery store plastic sweetened by a string of ribbon holding the blooms snuggly together. *Cute.* He must have picked them up on the way here. He was still trying to make an impression, even after calling me out the other day.

Maybe I shouldn't let this ship sail so fast.

I nodded toward the flowers and wryly asked, "Are those for me or for Jonie?"

"Jonie was just telling me about being stiffed by her last table," Nate explained. "And yes, they're for you."

"Oh, you work here?"

I turned to the side and squeezed between the two of them. Jonie made no attempt to get out of the way. I picked up the bouquet off the barstool, closed my eyes, and held it up to my nose. "These are beautiful. Thank you."

That was when I heard Jonie say, "Okay, well, it was nice meeting you—both."

"You good?" Nate asked again.

"I'm fine! Just had a long, crazy day, that's all."

"Crazy, huh? How so?"

"Traffic. That's all I meant."

"What's in Indiana?"

"There's a little shopping strip I'd heard about that's good for antiquing, bargains. No biggie. What's your day been like?" I asked, staring into his eyes so as not to be accused of not paying attention again.

"Are you sure you want to open that can of worms?"

"Of course. It had to be more interesting than antiquing."

"True. Most days I think I've got antiquing beat."

"Harsh," I said, only half joking. "Remind me not to share any of my other hobbies with you. What are you drinking?"

"I hope you don't mind. I ordered a cuvée before you arrived."

I hadn't even noticed the champagne bottle on ice by the window. "Here. Let me pour you some."

Isn't that supposed to be Jonie's job?

"Thank you. So, about your day . . ."

"Yeah, well, remember, you asked. *Crazy* doesn't describe the half of it. Cheers."

"Cheers."

Nate, not wanting the night to turn into the Jordan show, launched into what sounded like an episode of a television medical drama. He wouldn't be the first doctor to take pleasure in regaling others with stories from the ER. That's why there are so many hospital dramas. I hung on every word, changing expressions to match the highs and lows.

Who's performing now?

"Wow. All that in one twenty-two-hour shift? That's incredible." I reached across the table and touched the back of his hand. "Thank you for sharing that."

"You're welcome. Something's different about you."

"How so?"

"I mean, last time we were together, you barely noticed me."

I wanted to ask him so badly, "Can you just let that go? It was a group date." But he wasn't finished.

"Soft . . . thoughtful . . . kissable. I like this version of you."

"Who said I had versions?"

"Lady, you are Jekyll and Hyde," he said in a soft tone of voice that belied the critique. "I don't mean that in a bad way."

A couple of hours ago, I had the same notion, but it was definitely in a bad way.

"Uh, you do realize one of them is a killer, right?"

We laughed some more.

"I didn't mean it as an insult."

His face softened and the lines in his forehead smoothed, making him appear boyish. He inched in closer and rubbed my hand. I wanted to tell him that his job wasn't that much different from mine. We both dealt in life and death, and on any given day, somebody was not satisfied with our performance.

And people lie, don't they?

I understood now what Nate meant by his not being everyone's cup of tea. He was kind of an asshole, really. His form of attraction was a slow burn. If you could be patient enough to give him a beat or two to make up for it, you might end up at his apartment.

Nate took another opportunity to mention how busy he was. I wondered if he had ever dated someone he believed to be more successful than him, because he was constantly trying to amplify himself.

Is he intimidated by me?

"Man, if I didn't have to work so early tomorrow, I'd love to take you out to hear some music and just unwind."

"Next time."

"So there's going to be a next time?" he asked.

"I hope so."

Nate climbed down from the barstool and offered his arm to me. I laid the bouquet across my left arm and looped my right into his, like a bridesmaid in training. He walked me to the curb. As I raised my hand to hail a taxi, he gently lowered my arm and pulled me into an embrace. This hug felt different from the hug two hours ago.

"Thank you," he whispered and tightened his hold on me. I let him linger in the moment long enough to know he had my permission to go in for a good-night kiss—on the lips. He read my cue, kissing my right cheek, then my left, and finally my lips. And for once, I didn't talk myself out of giving in to the feeling and letting go.

20

Lieutenant Flanagan entered the interrogation room, a rookie cop whom Shelly had never seen before right on his heels.

"Good, I see you've calmed down."

"Where's my phone?" she asked.

"Ah, it's right here," said Flanagan, reaching into his left chest pocket. "I'm happy to return it to you."

"What are you holding me here for? I ain't done nothing."

"Miss Biltmore, it isn't my desire to keep you here. You are free to go."

Shelly stood up to leave, but Flanagan wasn't finished with her.

"What you're not free to do is spread lies about this department to the media. Clearly you gave this reporter—from *Chicago*—the impression that we didn't care about this case. Do you know how that makes us look?"

"I don't really care how it makes you look," Shelly said.

"Well, you should know that you're the one who's not looking so good right now. You didn't tell her about the liquor store video, did you?"

"I didn't tell her because I never saw that video," Shelly said, glaring at Flanagan, her back arched like that of a leopard about to strike. "You wouldn't let me see it, remember?"

"You knew of its existence," he shot back.

"And I'm supposed to take your word for it?"

"Miss . . ." Flanagan stopped himself. "Shelly, I don't know where all this distrust is coming from. But I have to tell you, the person getting in the way of this investigation the most is you."

"Oh, sure. Blame the victim."

"Interesting you would refer to yourself as the victim. I thought your sister was the victim."

"Lieutenant, don't try and twist my words."

"I don't trust you . . . Shelly. In fact, half of the men and women in this department struggle to trust you, and I think you know why."

"You people are no different now than you were then," she said.

"You're wrong!" said Flanagan, slamming his hand on the table, startling Shelly. She regained her composure, leaning back in her chair and giving him a cold stare.

"What you fail to realize is I'm the best you've got here. Now, you listen to me, I want to believe you about the bank video. I'm bringing in a specialist—a body language specialist."

"Body language?"

"Yes. She's going to compare the two videos we have to footage of your sister we were able to find on social media. She'll study her movements and physical characteristics, at least as much as we can make out on those tapes. From there, she'll make a determination about whether or not they match."

"They won't," Shelly said emphatically. "The woman on that video is not my sister. I swear it!"

"Well, we're going to get to the bottom of it. Now, you go on home, but I want you to think about something."

"What?"

"If the woman on that video does turn out to be your sister, then you're going to have to explain—no, you're going to have to convince me that you didn't get it wrong on purpose."

"Is that a threat, Lieutenant?"

"If you're trying to mislead investigators, Shelly, I *will* charge you."

Shelly huffed.

"Officer Fox, would you please escort Miss Biltmore to her car," Flanagan said.

Shelly rose from the small, unattractive table. "I can find my way." Stopping short of the door, she turned to face the policemen. "When's this specialist coming in?"

"She's already working on it. I should know something tomorrow."

"Fine."

"You're welcome," Flanagan said.

Shelly stumbled to her car as if she had been drinking. But in reality she had been physically and mentally drained by lack of food and sleep and the searing hatred she felt for Flanagan and, for that matter, the entire Jasper County sheriff's department. Two decades later, she was still paying for accusing a beloved ninth-grade history teacher, Mr. Colby, of touching her inappropriately backstage during a student assembly. Mr. Colby was put on unpaid leave pending an investigation. But before any conclusion could be reached, he purchased a .22-caliber handgun, parked his Lincoln Town Car on the side of Interstate 65, and ended it all. No one saw it coming. After that, whatever, if anything, happened to Shelly was inconsequential. She even started to doubt herself. Did she do something wrong? Had she provoked him? Maybe she misread his intentions, she confessed to a school counselor, who promised to keep Shelly's confidence but turned out to be indiscreet. A whisper campaign ensued, and Shelly was deemed an outcast and a liar by her peers and adults, alike. For years, she spiraled out of control. Drugs, alcohol, days-long benders. She was un-reliable, unhinged, and alone. Marla was indeed her only friend, who would one day face similar struggles of her own. Shelly thought it would bring them closer together. It didn't.

And though Shelly had beaten those demons, for the most part, thoughts of a substance like a 90 proof Kentucky Straight Bourbon Whiskey to take away the stress in moments like this were never far away. Shelly took a shortcut through the bank parking lot to Montesi's Liquors and pulled in front. There were two cameras on opposite corners of the building. One was angled toward the entrance, the other toward the parking lot. If Marla had walked into the store, as Flanagan said, surely the cameras would have captured her face.

Inside Montesi's, Shelly was startled by a shrieking voice.

"Shelly Biltmore!" said a woman from behind the counter. "Oh my god, how have you been?"

Shelly squinted to see this person who seemed genuinely happy to see her.

"Toni? Oh my god!" Shelly rushed toward the counter, where the woman greeted her with a tight, lingering hug.

"Oh man, it's good to see you," said Antoinette Strothers. She was one of four African American students in Shelly's graduating class. The warmth of her embrace felt like a tonic. It had been so long since anyone had held Shelly in their arms.

"What are you doing here?" Shelly asked. "I thought you were living out by Joliet. What's that town called?"

"Shorewood," Toni said. "I was, but my mom's not doing well, so I moved back to be closer to her."

"Oh, I'm sorry to hear that."

"Yeah, I'm sorry to hear about your sister. The police came

in here a couple weeks back asking to look at the security camera footage."

"Really? You were here then?" Shelly asked.

"Yeah. My manager pulled the tapes for 'em."

"Do you still have them?"

"Naw, they took them with."

"Did you see the video?"

"No, but my manager did."

Shelly wondered then what led police to check out Montesi's in
the first place. She questioned Toni like she was now the reporter.

"Who's your manager?"

"Her name's Maureen. I don't think you know her, though.
She moved here about five years ago. She married into Rensselaer. Her husband is on the police force."

"Sheriff's?"

"No, the local. And guess what?" Toni asked.

"What?"

"Hey, can I get rung up here?" said a man standing impatiently at the counter.

"Yes, I'll be right there! Hold on a minute, Shelly."

"I'm not going anywhere."

Shelly tapped her foot anxiously while she waited for Toni to
ring up the customer.

"Thank you," Toni said to the man, and walked back around
to the front of the counter.

"So what'd she say, Toni? Your manager?"

"She told me they were looking at surveillance video in a
missing person case. They didn't specify they were looking for
Marla, but after the story came out, I was convinced that's who
they were looking for."

"What else did your manager tell you?"

"She gave them the tape. But trip off this; she told me one of the sheriff's deputies was on the tape, too. He was getting into his car with a young woman, probably half his age. And on top of that, he's married."

"Who was it?"

"I've been gone for so long; I don't really know the local cops like that anymore. I think she said his last name was Barnes or Borden or something like that."

"Frank Barden," Shelly said matter-of-factly.

Toni responded, "Barden. Yeah, that's right!"

It was all starting to make sense. Flanagan didn't let her see that tape or release it to the media to protect one of his own.

"And you never saw the tape, right?"

"No," Toni said.

Maureen the manager likely had never seen Marla before and wouldn't have recognized her on the tape. So who did? It had to be Barden.

21

As satisfying as my date with Nate had been, I needed something stronger than a glass of bubbles to calm the anguish building inside me over Shelly's deception and Lin's relationship status. One tugged at my stomach, the other at my heart.

"Excuse me, can you pull over here?" I instructed the cab-driver, who overshot the Tiny Bar by half a block. I couldn't blame him. It got its name from the fact that it was about the width of the hallway in my apartment building and could hold only some fifteen patrons comfortably at a time. But it carried top-shelf liquor and an impressive array of tequilas. I set the bouquet on the last available table in the corner by the door to save my spot and sidled up to the bar.

"Hi, do you still carry Suave 35?" I asked the bartender.

"Yep."

"Great. I'll take a margarita on the rocks with salt."

As he filled my glass, it occurred to me how pathetic I must look, alone in a bar with a mixed bouquet from the corner store doing tequila shots. But this elixir helped clear the fog from my brain as I contemplated Shelly Biltmore's intentions and the lieutenant's reason for sharing just enough information to discredit her but leaving me with more questions than answers.

I caught the bartender's attention and held up a finger and mouthed, "One more." He nodded and pointed to his chest and then at me, indicating he would bring it over to the table this time.

The fact remained that a mother of two was still unaccounted for. And I was beginning to wonder whether the people closest to her really knew her at all.

"Hey there, lonely girl," the bartender said, smiling, as he sat another cocktail filled to the brim down in front of me. "This one's on the house."

Lonely girl was right; feeling a tad foolish, I said, "Thank you."

This drink I sipped and savored. I pulled out my cell phone to check my email and text messages. There were several no-tifications from the Facebook app and more than two dozen friend requests, including from my high school class and a true crime book club. I accepted the requests and perused the Class of '96 page, recognizing a few names from high school like the homecoming king and queen and a couple of cheerleaders, folks I hadn't thought about in years. On a different day, that might have brought me some joy, but right now, being stuck in the past was the last thing I wanted.

I didn't intend on being out until two o'clock in the morning, but late nights and early mornings were forming a habit, and I could feel the wear and tear from head to toe. It apparently showed on my face by the way Bass reacted when I stopped by the security desk after checking my mailbox.

"Jordie, are you okay?" said Bass, my brother from another mother and one of my dearest friends in this city. "You look tore up!"

Bass was the only man in my life who could get away with such a brutal critique. I didn't mind, though. We'd been through a lot together, to say the least.

"Thanks, Bass. You always say what a girl is dying to hear," I joked.

"Where have you been?" He smiled. "Hot date?"

"Yes, in fact. But that was earlier. I should've never started with the tequila shots and stuck with wine."

"Oh, so that explains why you're looking like that," he teased.

I wanted to say he didn't know the half of it, but my body craved sleep, and I was afraid I wouldn't get through the whole story without dropping to the lobby floor.

"So what have you got up to these days?" he asked.

"I'm anchoring next week."

"For real?" he said excitedly.

"Yep! I'm filling in on the morning show."

"That's awesome, Jordie! Should I say break a leg or something like that?"

"Yeah, that'll do."

"All right, woman, go to bed," he said. "Whatever it is, try and sleep it off."

I was happy to take that advice.

22

Saturday, March 21

I was in the middle of my third cup of coffee when the phone rang. It was Mom.

"Hey, sweetheart. I haven't heard from you in a few days, so I was just calling to check on you."

That role should be reversed, and I felt bad every time my mother, who lived alone, had to remind me that I was the one who was out of pocket and unreachable the majority of the time.

"Hey, Mom. I'm doing okay. I've been traveling this week for a story."

"Oh, where'd you go?"

"Not too far. Just Indiana."

"Okay. What are you working on?" she asked.

I would ordinarily dive right in to provide the gritty details, as my mother, unlike a lot of people, never grew tired of hearing about the crime stories I covered. Though my life as a crime reporter in a big city also kept her in a constant state of worry.

"It's a missing person case, but that's not the big news. Guess who I found on Facebook?"

"You're on Facebook now?"

"Yeah, believe me, I only signed up to do some research. But then I got nosy and decided to look up Lin."

"That's a name I haven't heard you say in a lo-o-ng time. I always liked Lin."

Mom used to say that every time I brought up his name after the breakup, which is why I stopped bringing it up.

"Yeah, Mom, I know. He's got a kid, a daughter."

"He's a military man," she said, as if that explained why he was a father. My dad also was a military man. Maybe she knew something I didn't.

"He's a lieutenant commander now."

"Wow, sounds like he's doing well. How long has it been?"

"About eight years."

"That's a long time. A person can change a lot in eight years. He's obviously moved on with his life, so no reason to be mad at you anymore," she said.

I had begun to hate the phrase *He's moved on*. I couldn't help feeling that the counterpoint to this was I hadn't.

"Maybe," I said. "Lately I've been wondering if I did the right thing. I just wish I could stop thinking about him."

"What started all that back up again?"

"It's this story I'm working on," I said. "Missing mother of two. It's strange, her sister tracked me down but she's not being totally honest with me. The woman's best friend doesn't think she's missing but that she just took off to get her head together. The woman is also going through a divorce. None of it makes sense."

To my surprise, my mother decided to forgo asking about the case and zoomed in on Lin. "You should send him a friend request," she said.

"I can't, Mom. I don't need that drama."

"Well, I'm on my way to yoga class," she said. "I'll talk to you later, Bae."

"Okay, Mom, love you."

"I love you, too, darling."

As soon as I hung up my cell phone vibrated on the kitchen counter. A text from Shelly.

Jordan, please call me back. I have some information, she wrote.

I felt something close to rage as I hit the callback button. I was about to read Shelly the riot act for not telling me about the liquor store video.

"Oh, thank god, Jordan! You won't believe what I found out last night."

"Shelly, frankly, I don't know that I would believe anything you tell me anymore."

"Flanagan got to you, but he's wrong."

"Why didn't you mention the security video from the liquor store? What else are you not telling me?"

"Are you giving up on me?"

"I don't give up on the truth. And it's not that I'm saying you're not telling the truth. But you can't help me or your sister if you keep leaving things out."

"I didn't mention the security video because I never saw it. I never corroborated that it was Marla on that tape. Did you ask Flanagan why he never released that video?"

"No, I didn't get the chance to ask him. He ended the call fairly abruptly," I said.

"He only did that to make me look like a fool. Trust me, that department has had it in for me since I was in high school."

Of all the oddities I had discovered about Shelly, this had

to be the strangest thing I had heard come out of her mouth. *Why would the police have it in for a kid? There must be one helluva backstory.*

"Why?"

"I'll tell you, but please, let me finish."

"Fine. Go ahead," I said, not trying to hide my growing impatience.

"I went by the liquor store last night. A friend of mine from high school works there now. She didn't see the tape, but she said her manager told her that the camera also caught a married police officer getting in his car with a young woman. They were clearly on a date. Don't you see? Flanagan didn't want that tape to get out because he's covering for this guy."

"If that's true, he should lose his badge. An internal affairs investigation would just be the start. But look, I need answers. Okay? What kind of run-in are we talking about, Shelly?"

Shelly exhaled deeply. Whatever it was, it was obviously not easy for her to talk about.

"Okay, I'll give you the CliffsNotes version. When I was fourteen, I reported my history teacher for touching me inappropriately. His name was Mr. Colby. Everybody loved him. He got put on leave, but then . . . then he committed suicide."

"Oh wow."

"Everybody blamed me. I was the most hated person in Rensselaer."

I'd sensed early on that Shelly's obstinance was the byproduct of some earlier event.

"The cop on the liquor store video, his name is Frank Barden. He and Mr. Colby were cousins. The whole community turned against me, Jordan. Everybody in my family suffered because of it. That's another reason why Marla wanted out."

I couldn't judge her for her omission. It wasn't the sort of thing you led with when you were trying to get someone to help you, especially in a matter of life-or-death.

"Shelly, I'm so sorry. That's horrible. But if Lieutenant Flanagan's motive for tiptoeing around this case was to honor the code of silence, that's deplorable."

"Oh yeah, he's a scumbag. But I think he's trying to help. He told me he was bringing in a specialist to examine both tapes to see if there are any similarities in the body language," she said.

"He's bringing in a body language expert. Interesting. But he still won't show you the liquor store footage?"

"He wouldn't budge on that," she said. "He knows my history with Barden. He's probably afraid I'll use it to hang his ass out to dry. But that's the last thing on my mind. Flanagan said he should know something sometime today," she said.

"All right," I said. "Let me know when you hear back."

I was relieved to know that Shelly hadn't deceived me, but troubled to find out the real reason the police had downplayed Marla's disappearance—to protect a cheating husband.

23

"Hello, this is Ron."

I could have called the main number at the dealership, but Ron Bridgeforth's card also listed a mobile number I opted for instead.

"Hi, Ron. How are you?"

"Uh, good. How can I help you?"

"My name is Jordan Manning. I'm a reporter for Channel 8 in Chicago."

Silence.

"What is this about, ma'am?"

His tone was defensive, a not-uncommon response. Was this some investigation about a bad car deal? Or a customer complaint that had now escalated?

"I'm looking into the disappearance of a Danville woman who might have been a customer of yours a few months back. Got a minute to answer a couple of questions?"

"A missing woman?"

"Yes, I think she may have been your customer."

"What's her name?"

"Hancock. Marla Hancock."

"Oh man, are you sure?"

"Yes. Do you remember her?"

"Yes! She was going through a nasty divorce."

I wasn't expecting that answer at all.

"How do you know about that? Did she tell you?"

"We talked and found out we knew some of the same people. Actually, she talked a lot that day about her marriage, her kids. I felt sorry for her."

Ron's defenses fell, and now all I could hear in his voice was shock and empathy.

"Sorry how?"

"She seemed desperate. I remember thinking, *Why is this woman telling me all this? Doesn't she have any friends?* But then she got a call, and I overheard her say something like 'When can I see the car?' I guess this woman had one for sale."

"What makes you think she was talking to a woman?"

"She was sitting at my desk at the time. I could hear their entire conversation almost. I even heard her say her name: Savannah."

"Are you sure?"

"Yeah, I'm sure. It's kind of an old-fashioned name you don't hear every day. It sticks with you. Marla asked to borrow a pen while she was on the phone. She wrote something on the back of my business card. Then she left."

"Ron, any chance you remember the month and date Marla was at the dealership?"

"I'm not sure of the exact date, but it was definitely around Halloween. She talked about her kids. I have a daughter around the same age as hers. It was all about the Princess Fiona costume. You know, from *Shrek*? I probably shouldn't tell you this."

"What?"

"She tried to buy a car that day. Her credit was pretty bad. Actually, she had no credit history at all, which is worse than bad credit. But it sounded like she had other options. Is the husband a suspect? Hey, you know they say it's always the husband."

"Ron, I can't go that far. I can only tell you she's missing, and her family called me for help. If you hear anything or recall anything else, will you call me?"

"Absolutely. Is this the best number on the caller ID?"

"Yes. This is my cell. Do me a favor? Text your name to this number so I can lock you in."

"Of course."

"Thanks for your candor."

"You're welcome. God, I hope she's all right. I thought she was cute; seemed like a nice girl. Do you think she's dead?"

"I pray that's not the case, Ron."

24

In the gaming world, you can be public or private. A little research helped me to at least understand at a base level how it all goes down. I soon realized there was an entire subculture I knew nothing about. A guy named Justin and a couple people he partnered with started Justin.tv. He began videotaping himself 24/7, kicking off something people started calling lifecasting, attracting millions. They literally wore cameras on their bodies and broadcast their day-to-day lives. I couldn't even imagine. No sooner did I think, *This could be a bad thing*, than I came across a news article about a young man who livecasted his suicide. My research left me with far more questions I needed answers to. It was like checking out what could be causing a rash on one of those medical websites and seeing diagnoses ranging from ringworm to a flesh-eating virus. Your mind is still left spinning.

Are you still following Jim online? I texted Shelly.

No, he blocked me.

Then how did you see his conversation with Hapinfast?

Did she figure out his password, too?

A picture my nephew took of action figures on top of Jim's desktop computer. He didn't mean to, but the screen was up.

A bizarre coincidence.
I'd left my reporter's notebook where Shelly wrote Jim's number in the car.

What's Jim's phone number again?

I wondered how Shelly was holding up after seeing the ATM video that wasn't of her sister. I was poised to text **How are you feeling today?** when my cell phone rang. It was Justin Smierciak, a freelance photographer and my extra pair of eyes and ears on the street. I clicked over just before the call went to voicemail.

"Justin! Where have you been hiding?"

"Hey, Jordie. Me hiding? I called you last night to see if you wanted to grab a drink. What? Were you on a hot date?"

"In fact, yes, I was."

"Well, excuse me."

"You're excused." I laughed. "What did you end up doing?"

"Just sitting around drinking beer, playing video games."

Justin and I had been close for four years, and it was surprising how little I knew about his private life, other than his obsession with video games, which I aided and abetted by gifting him a PlayStation 3 a couple of years ago as a thank-you for helping me stay ahead of the competition. It felt strange shopping for a game console for a thirty-year-old man, but who was I to judge? It's what he loves to do aside from chasing down news.

"Well, you always know what I need."

"What do you mean?"

"I'm working on a story that may have a video game connection."

"Really? Well, gaming cartridges are old-school. Live streaming is up-and-coming these days," he said. "Mark my words, a lot
of people are going to make a lot of money off this, and I'm going
to be one of them."

"I have no idea what you're talking about. But it's interesting.
This woman's sister showed me screenshots of chat messages on
some gaming platform. I'm trying to remember the name of it."

"Was it Justin.tv.?"

"Yep. That's it."

"What game?"

"I don't know. Hold on. I'll text her right now."

Shelly, do you know what game Jim has been streaming?

She wrote back immediately. **World of Warcraft is his go-to.**

"World of Warcraft. Do you know it?" I felt so out of touch
even asking based on Justin's judgy response.

"Do I *know* it? Jordan, where have you been? It's getting
kind of old now, though. It's been out for a few years."

"So do you hang out in the chat rooms?"

"Sure. I've met some people there, even a few who can play at
or near my skill level."

"Oh, so you're good?"

"What have I been telling you all these years?"

Perfect.

"How hard is it to find someone on these sites if you know
their username? It seems to be getting easier and easier."

"Not hard at all. All I have to do is type it in."

"I'm wondering if you can help me out. Can you spy on a couple people for me?"

"Uh, why am I spying on these people?"

"They may be involved in or know something about a Danville, Kentucky, mom who vanished about a month ago. I'll text you the usernames. Could we touch base tomorrow?"

"Okay, just text me when and where."

"Will do."

I stared at the back of Ronald Bridgeforth's business card. *Savannah. 2565 Manassas Ln.* Shelly was certain it was Marla's handwriting. Based on what Ron told me, I was now convinced that Marla had bought a car from Savannah. *Who is she? And does she have something to do with Marla's disappearance?*

My cell phone rang.

"Jordan, Flanagan called," Shelly said in a shaky voice.

"Oh no, Shelly, what's wrong? What'd he say?"

"The, um, body language expert? She says the woman in the liquor store video is quite possibly the same woman in the bank video. But she's certain that neither are Marla."

Shelly said what I was already thinking.

"I was hoping to God that she'd just lost it for a bit. That Victoria was right, she just needed a break. But now I know . . . somebody killed my sister. She's dead. I know she's dead."

25

Sunday, March 22

Multistate Effort to Find Missing Indiana Mom

(AP) RENSSELAER, Indiana—Police across three states are coordinating efforts in the ongoing search for a missing mother of two from Danville, Kentucky. Marla Hancock, 35, was last seen dropping her daughter off at a day care in Rensselaer on February 23.

Family members said Hancock, who is estranged from her husband, had moved back to her hometown and was looking for a job and an apartment when she disappeared. In a joint statement, Chicago and Illinois state police announced they joined the investigation over the weekend after learning that someone used Hancock's debit card to withdraw money from an ATM machine near downtown Chicago. However, according to a family member, the woman seen in the security camera footage is not her sister.

Mimi Maxwell had succeeded in keeping the story in the news. A piece she wrote about the investigation now being coordinated across multiple law enforcement agencies in Indiana, Kentucky, and Illinois was picked up by the Associated Press and appeared on page 3 of the Sunday *Sun-Times*.

I need to talk to you.

I texted Detective Joseph Samuels, my inside man at the Chicago PD, to see what he knew or was willing to help me find out. Then I shifted my attention online to see if I could locate Manassas Lane on the map. It's still amazing to me how Google Maps easily leads you right to the front door of someone's home. It's getting harder and harder to keep anything private or to hide. This is changing life and journalism. Once I typed in the address, within a couple of clicks, my cursor hovered over a modest white house with black shutters and three steps leading to a landing. The map showed the address was actually in Berea, not Danville. *What is that sign on the front door?* Magnifying it helped very little. Maybe it was one of those plaques engraved with the family name. I was trying to make it out when my concentration was interrupted by a phone call.

"Are you working today?" I asked.

"Slow down, slow down," said Joey. "How about 'How are you?'"

My friendship with Joey had long ago surpassed a reporter-source relationship. I trusted he already knew what was up when he saw my number. Some kind of request for a favor from me.

"I'm sorry. How are you, Joey? It's Sunday. I'm just trying not to take up too much of your time."

"Oh well, how thoughtful of you. And I'm well. What's going on?"

"I'm looking into the case of a missing Indiana woman. Marla Hancock. Do you know who I'm talking about?"

"Wait, you're working on it? How'd you know about that?"

"Oh, so you do know? You guys haven't said anything to the press."

"It's not up to us. This is interstate. The guys in Springfield are running the investigation."

"Really? Interesting. I found out because her sister literally tracked me down at the station. She told me Chicago PD shared an ATM video with her local sheriff's department, but she said the person in the video wasn't Marla."

I could sense Joey thinking over what I'd said through the phone. "What don't you know, Justice Jordan?"

"Plenty. That's why I'm calling you. Do you have any leads? Any suspects?"

"There's so many departments working on this thing now, it's getting a little frantic. But I heard police in Kentucky are taking a hard look at her husband and trying to ID the woman who used her debit card. She tried to use it again at a lingerie boutique on the North Side called Le Rouge Fleur."

Lingerie. I did a quick search for the store on my laptop. "There's two of them. Is it the one on North Clark or the one in the Water Tower?"

"Clark. 'Course there's no surveillance inside the store, and there's so much foot traffic up there, even if a camera *had* caught her leaving, we probably wouldn't have been able to ID her."

"You said she tried to use Marla's card?"

"Right, but it didn't go through."

"Did she try anyplace else?"

"Not so far."

"Did the card work at the ATM?"

"Now, that time it did. She withdrew the maximum—three hundred dollars."

"How long after did she try to use it at the store?"

"The next day."

Shelly mentioned Jim had cut off Marla's credit cards, but

he'd done that long before she vanished. Perhaps she had a low balance and the card was tapped out.

"Is it possible that it could've been Marla using her card?"

"Nothing conclusive yet, but the saleswoman at the lingerie store described this person as having dark hair. Marla's blond. But she couldn't tell us much more than that. It'd been weeks ago."

"Right."

"Okay, I've spilled all my beans. What do you have for me?"

"I don't know if it means anything, but I've got a name—Savannah. Has that come up yet?"

"No, who's that?"

"A friend of Marla's, but apparently neither her sister nor Victoria, her best friend, knew anything about her."

"Victoria Thatcher?" Joey asked.

"Yes. What do you know about her?"

"I know the Jasper County sheriff just named her a person of interest last week. I found out in the case briefing. Investigators said she acted strange during the interview."

"She acted like she'd had no contact with the police."

"You spoke with her?"

"Yes."

"Where?"

"At her house. Marla's sister, Shelly, took me by there."

"And you believed her? The victim was staying at her house, Jordan. That's the first place they went."

Victoria had outright lied to Shelly and me. What was she hiding?

"So now what?"

"There is no *now what*, at least not on our end, unless that card pops back up here again or we get some other lead."

"That's just so weird."

"There's a lot that's weird about this case. Up until now, police haven't been able to decide whether she's missing or hiding out someplace."

"You said up until now. So what do they think?"

"They're leaning toward foul play."

"Oh, one more thing," I said. "Shelly showed me a screenshot of a chat from a gaming site. It was between Jim and a woman who calls herself Hapinfast. But she also saw messages between Marla and the same woman."

"Maybe they were swinging," Joey said. "You know, people hook up on those gaming sites. They're the latest shell game in the sex trade. It's perfect because people don't have to show up as their real selves. They can hide behind an avatar and a fake name and do their dirt in plain sight."

I heard everything Joey said, but something clicked in my mind. "Oh my god! Now I'm starting to think that woman could be Victoria!"

"What makes you say that?"

"Shelly told me that Marla and Victoria had only recently reconnected. And in one of the chats, Marla said it was about time they met. But I bet Marla didn't know Victoria had been in touch with Jim."

"Sounds like deception," Joey said.

"Is that why Indiana police are looking at Victoria?"

"I don't know anything about the chat messages, but it makes sense."

If Victoria is talking to Jim behind Marla's back, I feel sorry for her when Shelly finds out.

"So how have you been?" he asked. "You okay?"

"Yeah. Hey! Guess what? I'm anchoring tomorrow."

"Aw, that's great, Jordan."

"Midmorning. Check me out."

"Are you running this story?"

"Why? Can I quote you?" I teased.

"You already know."

I had some decent leads in the case, but not enough to shed new light on the case or put it on the air. If I hadn't been scheduled to anchor tomorrow, I would have driven back to Rensselaer tonight to confront Victoria.

And you believed her? Joey's admonishment had stung. I'm sure he didn't mean to, but he made me feel like a novice. I thought Victoria was naive. Was I the naive one? It was all an act. I knew something was off about her, but I hadn't figured her to be an outright liar. At the same time, with her now in the sheriff's crosshairs, I wouldn't have expected her to volunteer that information if she was aware. Especially not in front of Shelly.

Can you do me a favor? Don't pick up Marla's clothes from Victoria's. Stay away from there for now, I texted Shelly.

Why? she wrote.

I'm still trying to figure some things out. But I promise, when I do, I'll let you know. Promise me you'll steer clear of her?

OK, but make it soon, Jordan. Something about that girl ain't right. I can feel it.

And where was Jim when all of this was going on? Did the police know? I dialed his number, but the call went straight to voicemail.

"Jim, this is Jordan Manning from Channel 8 News Chicago. I'm calling to ask you a few questions about your missing wife. Please call me back at 773-555-5698."

26

Le Rouge Fleur stayed open until five o'clock on Sundays. Parking was scarce in the trendy Lakeview neighborhood while the shops and restaurants up and down North Clark Street were still open. So I cabbed it there instead. Before I had even pushed open the door, I caught a whiff of a beautiful, almost overwhelming floral scent oozing from the entrance. It was overkill, yet added a bit of intrigue. I could see how a potential customer could be reeled in and seduced into buying something beyond the basic black staple bra. Inside, the lingerie boutique was quite modern. A long table of neatly folded loungewear almost dwarfed the room. The back wall was lined with more risqué sets of bras and matching bottoms. Nothing over-the-top—just sexy enough for Valentine's Day or a honeymoon. It was the kind of place I could fall in love with, not at all what I was expecting. I had pictured something more X-rated given this neighborhood's edge and the fact Le Rouge Fleur was next door to a tattoo and piercing studio. There was a small counter where the register rested on a smoked glass case with candles, body oils, and other last-minute temptations. Interestingly, there was only one salesperson on the floor, unless someone was working in the back.

"Hi there." A woman who appeared to be in her early twenties approached me. She was wearing lightweight wire-frame glasses and a vintage David Bowie T-shirt with a long black denim skirt. "Are you looking for anything special? Oh my god! Jordan Manning! *Hi-i-i-i!* I'm Britney."

Perfect! If Britney has answers, then the odds are already in my favor. She at least watches Channel 8 News, and from her greeting, she sounds like she likes me or my work.

"Britney, it's nice meeting you. Listen, I need your help. I'm working on a story and I'm hoping you or maybe one of your colleagues can answer a few questions off the record."

"Off the record?" she asked apprehensively. "Sounds serious. I should probably get my manager."

"No, no, it's fine. I just have a few questions you might be able to answer, that's all. Nothing big," I said, trying to keep Britney relaxed. I managed a smile.

"Look . . . um . . . Britney, some police came in here, oh, probably a week or two ago asking about a woman who attempted to use a stolen debit card that belonged to a missing woman. Do you recall that?"

"Uh, no. I must've been off that day."

Damn it! There goes my salesperson lead.

"You know, I think I should call my manager. This is above my pay grade. She's working in the storage area. Let me ask her if she knows anything."

"Okay."

I wandered toward the back of the store, where tucked away in the corner were shelves minimally stocked with accessories for shoppers looking for more than a sexy bra or a lace one-piece teddy to spice up their love life. *Oh wow*, I thought. Lace underwear with what certainly looked like a missing crotch and corsets with chokers attached. This wasn't the backdrop I wanted to have this conversation in, so I headed toward the checkout desk in front and noticed a statuesque woman walking in the same direction.

"Hi, Jordan. I'm Christina. Britney tells me you're doing a story on that missing mom. I was the one who spoke to the police, but I don't think I was much help."

"What do you remember about the woman who tried to use her card?"

"If I saw her again, I probably would recognize her. I remember she had long dark hair and she was wearing a big boxy coat. It looked like it was swallowing her. It was the color that struck me. This really pretty dark deep red, almost burgundy."

"So you ran the card, and it was declined. Do you remember what she was trying to buy?"

"Yeah, there were a few things. She had a couple of bra and panty sets with the matching garter belt. But we didn't have the size she wanted, so I told her I could order them and have them shipped. But like I said, the card was rejected."

"Wait, did you say she was wearing a red boxy coat?" said Britney, reacting as if a lightning bolt had struck her.

"Yes," her manager said.

"Was she looking at a cream and lavender set from one of our more expensive designers? The I.D. Sarrieri luxury line?"

"That sounds familiar, yes," Christina said.

"I waited on a woman who placed that same order, but she paid for it in cash."

"And it was shipped to her?" I asked.

"I think so. Yes."

"So you'd have a record of that, right?"

"Absolutely," Christina said. "I can search for the merchandise in our system, and that should pull up the order."

Both women moved around to the other side of the desk.

"While you do that, Christina, I'll check the drawer for the sales slip," Britney noted while looking at me. "We always keep a paper copy as a backup."

Britney griped, "These are in alphabetical, not chronological, order."

"Those receipts go back six months. That could take you a while," Christina said, her fingers darting across the keyboard of the desktop computer. "I'm pulling up the line now. Hold on."

"Okay, I think this is it . . . cream and lavender, size 8. Yes! The order was placed on February 27. See the date here?"

"What's the name on the order? And the address?" I asked.

Christina scrolled down. "It says here Marla Hancock, 2565 Manassas Lane, in Berea, Kentucky."

Wait. What? That's the address written on the back of Ronald Bridgeforth's business card. Is Marla alive after all?

"Can you print me a copy of that?"

Christina hesitated. "I'm not supposed to. But okay. Just . . . can you keep this confidential? I don't want to lose my job, but . . . Never mind, I'll do it."

"Don't worry. I would never reveal a source."

"Wait a minute," said Britney, drawing out each syllable. "I just found the paper copy for that order and it's under another name—Savannah Moultrie. Look." She handed her boss the slip.

"Let me check this against the stock number," Christina said. "Looks like it was shipped from our Water Tower store. Yep, the numbers match up!"

Britney pointed at the monitor. "Yeah, but the order in the system was placed on February twenty-seventh. The slip is dated the twenty-eighth. I wrote this up. This is my handwriting."

"So what do you think happened?" I asked.

Christina stood there, looking pensive, before finally throwing her hands up in the air. "Of course! I'd already written it up before the card was denied. I guess I forgot to cancel it out in the system," the manager said.

"Christina, that may have been the best mistake you've ever made."

27

I felt torn on the cab ride home. *Should I share what I just learned with Joey? With Shelly?* There were still so many unknowns. If Marla had tried to use the card at Le Rouge Fleur, why would the order be in the name of Savannah Moultrie? Was this woman, Savannah, involved in Marla's disappearance? Was she stupid enough to try and use Marla's card, then come back and place the order in her own name a day later? Or was Marla playing a game and using a fake name to throw the police and Jim off her trail?

I could go on the air with this. Couldn't I? There were standards. But it would have to get past legal and I wasn't sure it would. It was a one-source story at this point.

I pulled out a pen and my notebook and took a crack at drafting an intro.

As police in the tri-state area search for Marla Hancock ... missing Danville, Kentucky woman and mother of two Marla Hancock ... Channel 8 learned that someone, perhaps Hancock herself, tried to use her debit card at a lingerie store in the city's Lakeview neighborhood in late February. The charge was declined, but the next day witnesses say the same woman came back and placed a mail order, paying in cash under a different name—Savannah Moultrie.

If I'm right, Chicago PD doesn't have a clue about any of this.

The cab crept down Lake Shore Drive as traffic nearly came to a stop.

The woman in the video was described as having dark hair and wearing a boxy coat. The woman in the lingerie store also had dark hair and was wearing a boxy coat. There was little doubt in my mind they were one and the same. Marla? Someone else? Marla was blond, but if she was trying to disguise herself, that blond hair would be the first thing to go. *I have a choice to make. What's more important? Getting the story? Or doing what police have so far failed to do? Solve this case.*

I tried calling Jim again, but still no answer. I texted Shelly: **What's Marla's address in Danville?** and hoped my asking wouldn't spark a question I didn't have the answer to. Almost immediately my phone rang. I didn't recognize the number, but the area code was an Indiana one.

"Hello?"

"What did you tell the police about me?" said a woman's voice. She wasn't yelling, but I could tell from her tone she was on the verge.

"Who is this?"

"This is Victoria. Or was it Shelly who told them about me? I warned you about her! The police were at my house, and this time my children were here. Now they're crying and asking why the police want to talk to Mommy. My oldest asked if I was going to jail. I already told them I'd come to them, but no more stopping by my house!"

"Victoria, calm down. What are you talking about?"

"I'm sick of all of it! You hear me? I can't believe Marla put me in this position. She hasn't been honest!"

"Well, speaking of being honest, Victoria, why'd you lie to us about talking to the police?"

"I was trying to protect Marla."

"Protect her from *what*? The police? They're looking for her."

The police could have named Victoria a person of interest based on her bizarre behavior alone.

"I didn't want to say this in front of Shelly. You saw how unhinged she can get. But Jim told me that Marla was constantly threatening to leave. He said she was stealing money from him, too."

So Jim had noticed Marla's cash advances on the credit cards.

"He told me he thought she was using the money to feed her addiction. She even pawned a diamond bracelet that he gave her. I never got a chance to ask her about it because by then she was already gone, and . . . and . . ."

"What?"

"She was so different after she moved back home."

Her tone turned contemptuous. "And that friend of hers . . . Savannah."

"So you *have* heard of Savannah? Why didn't you tell us?"

"Marla asked me not to mention her to anybody, because Savannah was helping her out and she didn't want Jim to pick up on any clues after she left."

"Why was she so hell-bent on hiding from Jim? Victoria, I am confused by all of this. Was she afraid for her life? What is going on here?"

"I don't know. She'd never talked about her before, and I only met her that one time."

"And how long before Marla disappeared . . . or left?" *Even I'm not sure anymore.*

"It was the weekend before."

I pulled out my phone and checked the calendar. "The twenty-first. That right?"

"Yeah, I think so."

"For god's sake, Victoria, and you didn't tell the police?"

"Jordan, it's not like I'm trying to hide anything. I'm just as confused as everybody else. On the one hand, Jim seems to love Marla and wants her back home. But since she'd been hanging out with this new friend of hers, Savannah, I barely recognized Marla anymore."

"You know, Shelly said the same thing. That Marla was different. Tell me, how was she different to you?"

"Marla started to resent everything she'd ever done. Getting married, having kids, moving away from home. Jim had been cheating on her when she was pregnant with their second child. That really left her a mess. That's when the self-medicating started. It was all meant to ease the pain, but as you know, it made it worse. Jim told me he found her passed out on the kitchen floor one day. He threatened to divorce her and take the kids. That's when she checked herself into rehab."

"What was she taking?"

"It started with antidepressants and anxiety meds. Then later alcohol also came into play."

"And did that help?"

"It did for a little while. But Jim said he thinks she fell off the wagon after about six months."

"Sounds like you talk to Jim a lot."

"What makes you say that?"

"Well, Shelly told me that you and Marla had only recently reconnected. But it seems you and Jim were in contact long before Marla moved back to Rensselaer."

"No, that's not true," Victoria said defensively. "He only told me that recently."

"Oh. So what about you and Marla? Looked like you were close in high school."

"How do you know that?"

"She has several photos of you two on her Facebook page. And you have pictures of you and her when you were younger on your wall. So that's a fair assumption to make, right?"

"Yeah, of course."

"Did you two have a falling-out?"

"No! No, we just drifted apart, I guess. I was busy with my life, and she was busy with hers."

"Victoria, are you Hapinfast?"

"Am I what?"

"Do you use the screen name Hapinfast?"

"No, I've never heard of that. What are you talking about?"

Victoria could be lying or she could be telling the truth. Either way, I didn't trust her enough to tell her that Shelly had discovered the chat conversations Jim and Marla were having with the same woman.

"Now, where did you meet Savannah?"

"She came by my house that Saturday before. Marla told me she'd known her for some time and that she'd come to pick up her car."

"That's whose car Marla was driving?"

"Yes," Victoria said.

I knew it!

"Apparently, Marla was supposed to buy it from her, but she wasn't able to come up with the money. And the only reason I know that is because I overheard them talking. When she was here, I was in the den and I could hear them in the kitchen."

"What else did she say?"

"Savannah told her not to worry about the money for now. Just to keep the car."

"That's awfully generous. What was she doing in Rensselaer if she didn't come to take the car back?"

"When she introduced us, Marla told me Savannah was visiting family in Indianapolis, and since she was so close, she came by to check in on her. I told her she was welcome to spend the night. I offered her the couch in the family room downstairs. She thanked me but said she was staying at a motor inn in Kentland, about thirty minutes from here. I think this woman had a lot of influence over Marla. She was saying things like 'I know how you can make the money back. You can finally be single. Why do you want to live such a restrictive life?' Marla said something like 'I don't want to cause problems in your marriage.' And Savannah said, 'You can't. That's what's so great about being open,' and 'Remember what I told you?' I got the feeling she didn't want Marla and Jim to reconcile."

"I wonder what she meant by being open."

"I don't know what to think." Victoria started to cry. This was the sincerest she had been since I met her. "Like I said, I didn't know Marla anymore."

"What's the real reason that you believe Marla just took off? Tell me, Victoria."

"Just so you know, I feel like a traitor saying this," she said.

"What do you mean?"

"I know Shelly thinks Marla's this perfect wife and mother. That's what Marla wants her to believe, but that's not the person who showed up on my doorstep."

"Do you really think she walked away from her kids in the middle of a potential custody battle?"

"Marla told me she didn't want to be a mom anymore."

If this was a shocking revelation to me, I could only imagine Shelly's reaction.

"She said those exact words?"

"Yes. The worst thing a mother could ever say. *I don't want to be a mom anymore.*"

The most neutral person in this mysterious case, the victim's best friend, was also the most judgmental.

"Did Jim know?"

"If you're asking whether I told him, the answer's no. She's already dug herself a deep hole she may never be able to climb out of."

"What hole?"

Victoria paused and I held my breath while she thought about what to say next.

"I'm an idiot. What am I doing talking to a reporter? This is off the record, by the way."

"All right, Victoria. Fine. I'm listening."

"Marla told Jim she'd drop her petition for custody and let him have the kids. She just needed money to start over."

This is going to kill Shelly.

"I'm just hoping that wherever she is and whatever she's doing, that she gets help. But from the way Savannah was talking, it sounded to me like, if anything, Marla was about to get herself into a lot of trouble."

"What kind of trouble?"

"I don't know. Just a feeling I got."

"Have you talked to Jim lately?"

"No. Not in weeks."

"Wow, this is really complicated, isn't it?"

Even though Victoria had left out a lot of details before, I didn't believe she had anything to do with Marla's disappearance. Savannah, however, I was starting to believe did.

"Victoria, first, I never said a word about you to the police. Okay? And second, I appreciate you being honest with me now. But holding on to this information might have consequences."

"Are you saying I could go to jail?"

"I mean consequences for Marla. Police could have used that information to help locate her."

Silence.

"Look, Victoria, I've gotta go, but Savannah knows where you live. If she comes back around, call the police."

"Jordan, you've gotta believe me. I would never do anything to hurt Marla."

Elders in my family used to say, "Blood is thicker than water." Maybe if Marla had stuck it out at the farm with her sister, none of this would be happening. If I'd been in Marla's situation, I would hope my friends would do a better job of looking out for my welfare than Victoria had.

"I do believe you, Victoria." *The police, however, have doubts.* "But I've gotta go."

28

If Marla had faked her disappearance and was trying to lay low, why would she use her debit card, place an order in her name, then turn around and use a fake name and pay in cash?

Because it wasn't Marla. It was Savannah. And of all the things to buy with everything that was going on, why lingerie?

Shelly texted Marla's Kentucky address. **1690 Meadowood. Why?**

I'm going to do some digging.

I thought back to the chat messages Shelly showed me in the back office of the flea market between Marla and this person who went by Hapinfast on the gaming platform offering to help. "Whatever you need," she wrote. Was Savannah Hapinfast? Was it possible? *Are you kidding me?* Savannah and Jim . . . an affair? Or was something more insidious going on, like sex trafficking? If my suspicions were right, this was some bizarre triangle. Jim had betrayed his marriage vows before when Marla was pregnant. And if Savannah's movements were so easily traceable online, I was determined to track her not via the internet, but instead in the old-school way. I was going myself, in person.

Flights to Danville were not an option. The closest airport was in Lexington, Kentucky, almost thirty miles away. I knew that my decision could cost me a future shot at anchoring or even my job. I was risking it all for a woman I hadn't even met. I could just wait and let someone else take the lead. Why did I feel the need to take the risk?

"Hey!" said Ellen. "I'm surprised to hear from you on a Sunday. Are you excited about tomorrow?"

"That's why I'm calling. Ellen, I'm sorry, but I can't anchor this week," I blurted out with a faux confidence, certain I wasn't going to do it and fully knowing she would challenge this rash decision. "You're going to have to get someone else."

"Why? Are you sick?"

"I need to take some personal time off," I said, doubling down, signaling this was not up for debate.

"Are you okay? What's wrong?"

"I just need a few days."

"Wait. What's wrong, Jordan? Please tell me this isn't about that missing mom case."

While this decision was not up for debate, my vagueness was not helpful. No way Ellen was going to accept my bowing out without a detailed reason why.

"Someone tried to use her debit card at a lingerie shop on the North Side."

"Jordan, you don't just bail out on an opportunity like this! Are you insane! I can't believe this. If you didn't want to anchor, why'd you agree to do it?"

I hadn't expected her to ask me that, but it was the right question. The only way to deal with it was to play the best card I had left in the deck.

"Ellen, anchoring isn't my dream; it's everybody else's. At least not yet. I'm an investigative reporter with a reputation for being relentless about getting the story. That's what the Justice Jordan promo is all about, right? Otherwise, it's just some corny slogan."

"Look, you blindsided me with this."

"It's like marriage. I'm going to want that one day, but not yet. And who knows? Maybe I'll decide marriage isn't for me, either. I've got to live for now—for me."

I knew it was only seconds, but it felt like minutes before Ellen spoke. "How long are you asking for?"

"Three days."

"Three?! Do you have anything you can file right now?"

I could. But I won't.

"I'm really close, but I need a source to go on the record."

"You're trying to break this case, aren't you? Because if you had something verifiable that we could put on the air, you would've told me. You're going rogue again."

If we hadn't already been down this road before, I would have been more sympathetic toward Ellen in her position. But if you didn't know me by now . . .

"Here's what I can tell you at this point. I think Marla Hancock got caught up in a love triangle and things didn't end well. And now someone is trying to cover it all up."

"What do you mean?"

"A woman tried to use Marla Hancock's debit card to buy lingerie. She's a friend of hers. I was able to ID her. Why she was using her card leads me to nothing but red flags."

"I don't follow," Ellen said.

"Was using the card sloppy or intentional to throw off police? I covered a story back in Texas involving a missing twenty-nine-year-old woman named Esmeralda Diaz. Her boyfriend, Dwayne Verde, was a lot older. At the time he was forty-one. Dwayne planned and carried out an elaborate lie to make it look like she had been abducted. He ransacked her apartment and called in ransom demands from pay phones in five different cities. He went on the air and pleaded with her alleged kidnappers to release her unharmed. He hung around her parents' home and pretended to try and come up with the ransom money—$500,000. It was an impossible sum for the family to raise and he knew that. When the ransom calls suddenly stopped, the Diaz family lost hope that Esmeralda was still alive. With no leads, Verde figured law enforcement had given up the search, not realizing he'd been a suspect the entire time. Police tracked his movements for weeks. Then one day, feelings of guilt and remorse must have gotten to him, because while the police were following him, he led them to an area where they searched and found her body. He thought she was cheating and strangled her to death. Detectives always suspected he was aware he was being followed and knowingly led them to the spot."

"So that's what you plan to do? Track this woman down?" she said. "If she is a suspect, don't you think the police could be tracking her, too?"

"No, because I don't believe they've connected the dots yet. Ellen, just trust me, okay? I've got a solid lead."

"Jordan, this is not ethical. You've got to turn this over to investigators."

"Ellen, like the Diaz murder, the circumstances surrounding Marla's disappearance feel the same, but I don't know that I have enough proof. I can't go in and accuse an innocent person of the crime, which is why I have to go."

"Then you'd better get me something I can put on the air."

29

Monday, March 23

Berea was a little over six hours from Chicago. Driving made more sense. I set my alarm for three A.M., filled a large thermos with coffee, and was speeding down a near-empty Illinois toll road by four. It was the same route I'd taken a couple of days earlier to Rensselaer. I made it to Indianapolis just as the sun came up and was scanning the car radio for a clear station when a call came in.

"Hello?"

"Hello, Jordan. It's Mimi Maxwell. I hope it's not too early."

I hadn't expected to hear from Mimi this morning. I was a little concerned because she sounded out of breath.

"No, it's fine. Are you okay?"

"I'm good. Great, actually. My piece ran yesterday about the ATM video that proved it wasn't Marla, and how police in three states are now involved in the probe, and it's going nuts!" she said in one breath.

"What do you mean, going nuts?"

"It's getting great pickup. I just got an email from CNN! They want to interview me! It's all over the morning shows."

Did I just get beat on this story by a rookie reporter? I fought hard not to sound too stunned by this revelation. "I did see the story in the Sunday paper. Did you get a police source to go on the record yet?"

"No, I attributed it to 'a source with the investigation.' Trust me, it wasn't easy to get my editor to agree to that one."

"Okay, I'm driving right now. Can you let me know if you post an update?"

"Sure, no problem. Hey, when are you airing your story?"

"Soon. I don't know exactly when. The link to Chicago may be evaporating."

"Oh, okay, got it."

"By the way, Mimi, incredible reporting."

And to think, that could be me getting a call from CNN. But instead I'm here.

"Thanks. I appreciate that, Jordan. Okay, well, I'd better respond to CNN." She laughed nervously. "I'll keep you posted."

"Right. Talk soon."

Law enforcement's reluctance to go on record didn't make sense to me at this point. Were they afraid of tipping off whoever was posing as Marla? Were they closing in on a suspect? Or were they trying to freeze out the media?

My phone started to ring nonstop with text messages from friends and colleagues. I didn't have to guess why.

Hey what happened this morning?

Did I miss you anchoring?

Thought you were anchoring. Did I get the day wrong?

Detective Joseph Samuels didn't text but called.

"Hey, Joe, what's up?"

"Weren't you supposed to anchor this morning? It sounds like you're driving."

"I am. I didn't anchor. I pulled out."

"Why? Where are you headed?"

I sighed, bracing for his admonishment. "Kentucky."

"What are you trying to do?" Joey had that familiar sound of exasperation in his voice. "You can't beat the cops to the story."

"I wouldn't be so sure. Marla's been missing for almost a month now. They can follow their leads; I'll follow mine."

"I don't have to tell you how dangerous this could be. This woman could be dead, and you could be walking right up to her killer."

"I'll be careful. I promise. I won't do anything outside the light of day."

"Jordan . . ."

"Come on, Joey. Work with me on this. I promise, I'll let you know about anything I find out."

"Technically, this isn't even my case. What are you looking for in Kentucky?"

"Remember I told you about Marla's friend, Savannah? I went to the lingerie shop. I think Savannah tried to use Marla's debit card but came back the next day and paid for the same order in cash and had it shipped to her address."

"I heard our boys talked to the manager there. Marla's name was on the order."

Why hadn't he mentioned that before?

"I know. But they should've gone back and questioned other employees, because a clerk who worked the next day waited on the same woman."

"All right, listen, you be careful. It's not like Danville is up the street. If you get into trouble, I won't be able to help you."

Joey had known me long enough to know that when I was in this deep, when I was this close, I was like a dog with a bone.

"I'll keep my distance."

Halfway to Berea, I needed a distraction to drown out the noise in my head and remembered that I owed Lisette a call.

"He-e-ey." She yawned.

The early hour had slipped my mind. "Girl, I'm sorry. Did I wake you?"

"Uh-huh. Look at you, acting like Jenny B.," she teased. "And why haven't you RSVP'd for the shower? Hello?"

"Uh, wait, I thought I did. What's the date?"

"Really, Jordie? It's Easter Saturday."

Liz had every right to be annoyed with me. I had seen her email reminder but never opened it. It was official: I was the lamest maid of honor in history. As it was, her little sister had made most of the arrangements.

"Remember?" she pressed.

"Look, I figured my RSVP was assumed, since I'm a VIP."

"Exactly! You're my VIP. So no playing cops and robbers that day. I can't believe you forgot the date."

"No, no . . . Of course I didn't forget."

"Okay, get on it!" demanded Liz, her inner bridezilla showing. "Jordan, I'm happier than I've ever been. It's important to me that the people I love share in that happiness. Jordan? Did you hear me? Are you doing something right now?" By her tone of voice, I could tell Liz was increasingly frustrated with me.

"Liz, we've been over this. Of course I'm happy for you. What are you talking about?"

"You seem distracted. Actually . . . I hate to say this, but . . . you've been a little distant lately. And that's not how I imagined this going. You're my best friend. I chose you to be my maid of honor over my sister, for goodness' sake. I still haven't heard the end of that."

Liz sounded as if she had forgotten the angst I shared with her about Lin and being uncoupled at the big event just a few days ago.

"I know. I am your best friend . . . who happens to disappoint people a lot. I'm sorry."

My chat with Lisette wasn't turning into the morale boost I needed. It was out of character for me to play the martyr. But here I was doing it for the second time in a week. She was right, though. Being forgetful and not fully present in people's lives were shortcomings of mine Lin talked about, and I didn't know what I had to do to fix them. Yet here I was driving over three hundred miles to find out what happened to a woman I'd never met.

"I'm not trying to make you feel bad," she said, "just reminding you how important you are to me. You've been there with Mike and me from the beginning. I know you're struggling with Lin demons right now. And I sympathize. But you're family, and now Mike's going to be your family, too."

I would have told Liz about how memories of Lin had continued to haunt me these past few days. But the selfless thing for me to do would be to keep any negativity about romantic relationships to myself.

"And I'm looking forward to that, Liz, really I am."

"I want for you what I have," she said. "Love."

Please do not launch into another "he's out there" speech.

30

Monday, March 23
10:06 A.M.

The Garmin GPS directed me to take the next exit onto a Kentucky state highway for the final leg of the trip to Berea. Known for its hiking trails and art festivals, this area had some breathtaking landscapes. Beautiful vistas overlooking a river winding through green rolling hills burst into view between patches of dense forest. Finally, at Manassas Lane, the highway abruptly ended and curved to the right past the white house with the black shutters. The obscure letters on the sign over the door were hard to make out even this close. The neighborhood bordered a campground and recreation area. As for a spot to stake out the house without drawing attention, a nearby picnic area with wooden tables and in-ground barbecue pits would have to do. It was thankfully empty this time of day, so I pulled into a parking spot facing the backyard. The house didn't have a garage, but there was a car parked on a concrete slab where a garage used to be. A late-model Buick Regal would be my guess. It was 10:15. This could turn into one long day of waiting.

A makeshift driveway of dirt and grass lay between me and Manassas Lane. The houses were well spaced out, not on top of each other. The nameless subdivision might have started as a haven for new home buyers and young families with small children. But now, from the looks of it, the kids were grown and gone, and their parents were settled into a quiet, comfortable nonflashy way of life. The contrast between this area and Victoria's neighborhood of sanitized suburban simplicity was striking. An elementary school was a short walk away. There were no manicured lawns, colorful flower beds, or neatly trimmed bushes lining the property. No cul-de-sac provided a bit of privacy or even a faux sense of safety.

Only thirty minutes into the stakeout, I felt my patience give out. I got out of the car and walked down the hill to a sidewalk running along the length of the block. Walking past Savannah's backyard through a low-lying grassy pathway, I prayed no one saw me or, worse, called the cops to report a woman skulking around their neighborhood. Holding my cell phone to my ear and pretending to be just another neighbor, I doubled back toward her house and could finally make out the sign above the front door: The Moultries. It, too, had seen better days.

Oh, Savannah. You have been sloppy, haven't you?

• •

I'm sure you know by now the lid's off this story, Ellen texted. So you'd better bring something home soon.

It was a warning, not just from Ellen but from the general manager. I knew she couldn't keep covering for me forever with him breathing down her neck.

Contact our Danville affiliate to see if they can lend us a camera or recommend a freelancer, I texted.

En route to my car, I took the long way around to avoid

suspicion and was about to cross the dirt drive up the hill when the muffled sound of a man and a woman arguing stopped me. About ten yards away, the heated conversation became clearer after the back door to the Moultries' house flung open and smacked against the house so hard it sounded like a gunshot. Both people were yelling.

"I can't believe the mess you've got me into!" a man said.

"You can't blame this on me, Sterling! You weren't even supposed to be there!" she shouted.

"Whose fault is it, then? Hers? She was innocent! You went there to meet him and got caught!"

"I wasn't meeting him! I told you I ended that a long time ago!" she said, her voice racked by emotion.

"You're lying! You're the reason I'm in this situation. All you had to do was stick to the plan. This is all your fault!"

"No, you got us in this mess because you couldn't take care of us!" she shot back. "Everything I've done, everything you've put me through . . . what kind of man does that make you?"

A visibly shaken Savannah bolted out the back door with a backpack slung over one shoulder. She ran toward the car, nearly falling over a bag of mulch lying in the driveway.

The man she referred to as Sterling appeared in the doorway. "Where are you going?" he demanded.

"Stay away from me!" she screamed.

"Don't I at least have a right to know where you're going?"

"Go to hell, Sterling!"

Savannah tossed the backpack in the passenger seat of the Buick.

I ran up the hill as fast as I could, but by the time I got in my car, Savannah had sped off. I hit a quick U-turn and struck out in the same direction she had gone toward the state highway. I soon came to a fork in the road. I could go left to enter the freeway or go right to take the outer drive. Savannah already had a head start. Figuring that catching up to her on the freeway, at this point, was out of the question, I made a split-second decision to hang right onto the outer drive and got held up at the first traffic light. Fortunately Savannah had chosen to go right and had gotten held up there, too. Sitting two car lengths behind her, once the light changed, I followed her onto the two-lane Kentucky state highway before she exited onto the four-lane U.S. interstate toward Danville, making it perfect for me to follow more discreetly.

Dear God! I'm actually trailing someone. But that's what I came here to do. After about six miles, Savannah took the off-ramp and turned into a shopping center with a Hallmark card shop, a GNC health store, and a Carter's kids' outlet. She drove behind the mall and parked in front of a lone three-story brown-brick building, a medical center. I parked between two cars that put me close enough to see exactly where she was going. Just in case I'd been spotted, I waited a couple of minutes before going inside. I had no idea how real detectives tailed people, but I was certain my nerves were far more frayed than theirs would be.

"Sign in, please," said a female security guard sitting behind a desk in the lobby. Savannah had signed in and listed her destination as suite 360 on the log. "Where are you headed?" the guard asked.

"Uh, suite 360."

"Dr. Young. Michael Young," she said.

I nodded in agreement.

The guard wrote something down on a cardboard tag with a clip attached and handed it to me.

"Here you go. Just keep this on you and drop it off at the desk before you leave."

"Thanks."

I had no idea what to expect. The elevator stopped on the third floor, Dr. Young's suite. The waiting area was filled with women, many of them in various stages of pregnancy. I took a seat closest to the reception desk. Savannah was standing there behind one other woman waiting to check in. Her long dark hair, swept messily to one side, was in need of a good brushing. Even from behind, I could tell her breathing was rapid by the way her shoulders rose and fell under the striped knit jersey clinging to her toned, athletic physique.

"Savannah Moultrie. My appointment was for eleven-thirty. I'm sorry, I'm running behind. I had some car trouble."

"No problem. The doctor had a delivery this morning, so he's running a little behind himself. Babies come first! You'll appreciate that when it's your turn. You're here today for your three-month checkup?"

"Yes, that's right."

I couldn't believe how loudly the receptionist was speaking in a setting governed by privacy laws. Three-month checkup?

"I see that we don't have a copy of your insurance card."

"I've been paying in cash," Savannah said.

"Okay, I'll need to get that from you now. That'll be $250."

Savannah reached into her backpack and pulled out an envelope that she slid under the service window.

"Bring the form up when you're done, and see the door to my right? A nurse will meet you on the other side to get blood and urine."

Savannah disappeared behind the door, and I walked over to the wall-mounted magazine rack and picked up an issue of *People* magazine. There was a separate rack with pamphlets on various topics—breastfeeding, even cord blood storage—and what appeared to be every issue of *Parents* magazine from the past year. *She's pregnant!* Everything I had learned about this woman so far didn't add up. On the one hand, she was gracious enough to loan Marla her car so that she could escape her tumultuous marriage. On the other hand, she had been buying lingerie with Marla's debit card. Now this? Who was the real Savannah?

It was a little under an hour before Savannah reemerged from the exam room and headed back to the reception desk. She declared, "I need to pick up my prescription."

"Yes, I have it right here in this folder with a couple of brochures."

Savannah smiled and fussed with her hair. Her fingers were unusually long, almost bony and with no rings, just how Shelly had described the woman in the ATM video. There was no doubt in my mind that the woman in the video and the woman at the lingerie store were the same. Did Savannah kill Marla? But why? Because she was having an affair with her husband? Could she be pregnant with Jim's child?

"I've picked out a name," she told the receptionist, unsolicited.

"You know what they say. It's bad luck to share," the woman replied.

"Baby Jesse will never have a bad day in her life with a father like hers," Savannah said.

"We'll see you back here at twenty weeks," the receptionist said politely.

Savannah left the clinic and headed toward the elevators just outside the door. I grabbed a breastfeeding brochure on the way out.

"Excuse me. Excuse me," I said as I approached her. "You dropped this."

"Oh," she said, looking over the brochure, slightly confused, not recognizing it as her own. "Thanks."

This was my chance to make my move. Did I blurt it out and tell her who I was? Did I ask about Marla? Or let her know that the police might be one step behind, but I wasn't?

31

I've got something. Call me. Can't text this.

It was Justin. I'd nearly forgotten I had asked him to see what he could find out about Jim and Savannah on the gaming platform. And as badly as I wanted to hear what he had to tell me, I didn't want to lose Savannah when I was this close. I left the clinic a couple of steps behind her and contemplated riding down on the elevator with her but decided to keep my distance and take the stairs. Exiting on the side of the building, I saw her just as she was getting into her car. *Oh no! What's going on?* I could see Savannah resting her head on the steering wheel, at one point clearly wiping away tears.

What had changed from her earlier unsolicited presentation of possible names for the baby?

A message came in from Ellen. I've got a camera from the local. Where should he meet you? She clearly wasn't going to ease up on me until I got her a story, and too impatient to allow me time to respond, she called.

"Ellen. Hey!"

"Did you get my text?"

"Yeah, I just read it."

"Listen, I wanted you to know the victim's husband is a dead end. He's refusing to talk to the media, and from what I could tell from the cable news coverage, reporters are waist-deep outside his house right now. So if you're not already there, then you're too late."

"I figured I wouldn't be missing anything there. I've been leaving messages for that guy for several days. The call goes straight to voicemail," I said.

Mimi was right. Not only was her story getting a lot of traction, but it had also ignited a media frenzy.

"Ellen, this is so messy. I found Savannah. She's pregnant!"

"What? How do you know that?"

"You have to trust me. Something I saw. Okay? It's undeniable. And she's having an affair. I told you I thought Marla got caught in a love triangle. I can't prove it yet, but I think Savannah's been sleeping with Jim Hancock, or at least she was."

"That's motive right there!" Ellen said.

Ellen sounded more like a detective than an editor. Maybe I was starting to rub off on her.

"What's your next move? Sounds like you're driving. What about the camera?"

"Let's wait on that. I'll keep you posted."

"Please, please, be careful. I don't have to remind you . . . be a journalist, not a cop."

"Yeah. Okay, I've gotta go."

Savannah was on the move. She drove around to the front of the shopping center, parked, and went into the children's outlet store, providing me with a window to call Justin.

"Hey, Jordan. I don't know what kind of freaky story you're following, but I hope you're sitting down."

"Why? What's up?"

"I've got nothing on rubble&rock. Looks like he hasn't been playing on the platform for a few weeks."

"Well, the mother of his children has been missing for around that much time."

"I found your girl Hapinfast, though."

"Really?"

"Yeah."

"Did you get her real name? Let me guess. Is it Savannah?"

"It is. I told her I'm from Chicago, and she said she was just in Chicago."

"Wait! You spoke to her?"

"We text in the chat. She was flirting big-time, and not just with me but with other guys in the chat, too."

"How do you know that?"

"It's a big community, but at the same time, it's small. Okay? A whole other world. A lot of things go down. People make friends, go into business together, they hook up . . ."

"What? Like go on a date?"

"Not a date," he said, amused by my reaction. "She was flirting with a lot of guys, trying to get them to meet up in person. Know what I mean? One of my friends was in the chat, too. When he noticed us writing back and forth, he sent me a private message and was like, 'Dude, you do not want to go there.'"

"What did she do?"

"I just emailed you something he sent me from her."

"Okay, hold on." The attachment downloaded slowly, but right away I was taken aback by the image. A woman in a provocative pose wearing a black lace teddy.

"Oh my god! That's her! What the hell?"

"Right? He loved the flirting and was ready to hook up. But when she lowered the boom that it would cost him, he was out. She's soliciting, Jordan. She said she'd meet him for four hundred dollars."

"Where does your friend live?"

"Indianapolis."

Is that why Savannah was in Indy? My mind was completely blown.

"Is she in trouble? In danger?" Justin asked.

"Honestly, I'm not sure. Maybe both. Good work, Justin! Listen, I've gotta go. I'll contact you later."

There was no longer any doubt in my mind that Jim and Savannah hooked up after meeting on the gaming site. And one or both of them wanted more after that. It's like Ellen said—that's a motive to commit murder. It's always the husband. That's the prevailing theory when a wife disappears. And by the way, we know from the stats it's true. Viewers at home watching the news or one of those crime shows are always suspicious of the man in the picture. But this time, the husband may not have acted alone. Jim didn't want to financially support a wife who had fled, and Savannah, catching a glimpse of the life Marla seemed no longer to appreciate, was eager to take her place. Maybe Savannah was in fact meeting Jim, and he used her to set Marla up. Then there was Sterling. His wife's infidelity wasn't news to him, but did he know she was prostituting herself? *You went there to meet him and got caught,* he'd accused her. My instincts were telling me that Sterling, like Guillermo Morales, might be the most vulnerable of all the players, though, unlike Morales, not in ways that would lead him to commit cold-blooded murder. If Jim or Savannah turned up missing, he would be my lead suspect. However, he had no reason to harm Marla. *But if I can get him to crack, then maybe I can crack this case.*

32

While Savannah shopped, I decided to use this time to try and talk to her husband before she returned home. With the media staking out Jim's place, it would be risky for Savannah to go there or for the two of them to meet in public. She could be back hours from now, or, with no further errands to run, within minutes.

Manassas Lane was dead silent. No neighbors tending their yard or taking a stroll. Would I have felt more comfortable with a cameraperson present? Absolutely. But the odds of Sterling's opening the door and letting me in with a camera pointed at him were slim to none.

I parked in front of the house, and the moment I got out of the car, a blast of the wintry chill that regularly showed up during the Midwest's early spring hit me like a thousand tiny needles pricking my skin. My adrenaline was at peak level as I walked up to the house.

On the way I had an unnerving thought: *Nobody knows I'm here.* I snapped a picture of the house on my phone, making sure to capture the address and the sign over the door, and texted the image to Joey. On Manassas Ln in Berea KY. Will explain later.

Seconds after I rang the doorbell, Sterling came to the door in his bare feet, wearing a sleeveless sweatshirt and jeans. His thick eyebrows made him appear more serious than he probably meant to look at times. His hair slightly receding at his temples, he was ruggedly handsome. Tattoos covered his entire left arm.

"Can I help you?"

I cleared my throat, now dry from the anxiety that had been building as I approached. "Hi, my name is Jordan Manning. I'm a reporter for Channel 8 News in Chicago. I'm sorry to interrupt, but can I talk to you for a moment?"

Sterling's face turned white as chalk and his Adam's apple protruded as he swallowed hard. "Chicago? What do you want?"

We both were showing signs of stress, but I was guessing for far different reasons.

"It's about Marla Hancock. Can I come in?"

"Who? I don't know who that is, and no, you can't."

"Marla Hancock? From Danville? She's missing. It's been all over the news."

"Never heard of her," he said.

"It's my understanding that your wife let her borrow one of your cars and that she was one of the last people to see Marla before she disappeared."

"Look." He shook his head. "You're mistaken. You've got the wrong family. Excuse me."

Sterling was about to shut the door, but I stepped in closer, using my body as a barrier. I knew that getting him to talk wasn't going to be easy, but this was a bold but risky move that now made reasoning with him potentially out of the question.

"Lady, what the hell's your problem?"

"Sterling, listen to me. This is important. Your wife is mixed up in this somehow. Please. You're about to be a father yourself, so I'm sure you can understand and appreciate what Marla's family and her children are going through."

His demeanor suddenly changed from angry to incredulous.

"What'd you say?" Sterling's voice went up an octave and cracked. "About to be a father? Lady, you're crazy. There are no babies on the way here."

Sterling doesn't know Savannah's pregnant, which means either the child isn't his or Savannah's keeping it hidden because she isn't sure who the father is. Think, Jordan!

With the tiniest window of opportunity remaining to keep him engaged before he slammed the door in my face, I needed to figure out a way to trigger him.

"Savannah was caught on video trying to use Marla's debit card. Oh, and the new lingerie, has that arrived yet? She had it shipped here from Chicago," I said.

Sterling, visibly rattled, looked like a bomb went off in his head. "Who told you to talk to me?" he stammered. "Was it Savannah? What'd she say?"

"No one sent me. And I haven't spoken to your wife. But I do know some things."

A door slammed. The noise came from the back of the house. Sterling turned his head slightly toward the back. "Savannah! Get up here!"

Time wasn't on my side.

"Sterling, whatever it is . . ."

"Get up here now!" he demanded.

"What?" she responded, annoyed. "Who's at the door?"

Sterling opened the door wide, and Savannah looked like she had seen the devil.

"You! Are you following me? What are you doing at my house?"

"You know her?" Sterling asked.

"I saw her . . . earlier today."

Knowing where she was earlier today, Savannah rushed toward me. "Ma'am, you have got to go!" Gripping my upper arms in a vise hold, Savannah pushed me backward, then leaned in, her lips to my ear. "You need to leave here!"

Did she just put her hands on me?

She backed away. "I already told you I don't know anything. You could've called first."

"Wait!" Sterling looked directly at me. "Do you know each other?"

"I don't know her," Savannah said, "but I think she's following me."

"Just hold on." Sterling pulled Savannah inside and partially closed the door, holding it slightly ajar. I could hear him whispering loudly, "She's a reporter!"

"What?" Savannah muttered.

"Savannah, I came here to ask you about your friend Marla Hancock," I said, craning my neck around the half-closed door.

"What are you doing?" Sterling asked Savannah. He wasn't directly in my line of sight, but I could still hear him.

Savannah reappeared at the door. "Who are you? What is this about?" she asked.

"Jordan Manning, Channel 8, Chicago."

"How do I know you're a reporter?" she asked.

I reached inside my bag and offered her my card. She glanced but didn't want to even examine it or touch it, for that matter.

"I was just explaining to your husband that you might know more about a missing person case I am covering. Marla—I think you know her pretty well."

Savannah stayed silent, but her expression morphed into a hard, frightful stare.

A thousand alarms must be going off in her head. She tossed her hair and forced a strained smile, regaining some of her composure.

"You're not the cops. I don't have to talk to you," she said and turned her back to me.

"You have a lot to explain, Savannah. I'm sure the police will be talking to you real soon. Or you can go on the record and explain your side of things. If you've done nothing wrong, this can all be cleared up."

She snatched the card out of my hand, stomped back into the house, and slammed the door.

33

The clock was winding down. I had two more personal days off. Up since three o'clock, I needed to get some sleep. The Super 8 near the Danville-Berea border was only five minutes from Savannah's house. If she changed her mind about the interview, I wanted to be close by with a camera crew on standby.

I passed out, and when I finally woke up and checked my phone, it was after nine o'clock. My voicemail was full on top of eight unread text messages. Savannah wasn't the only one who had some explaining to do.

Staying overnight. Talk tomorrow, I texted Ellen then walked over to the nearby Cattleman's Roadhouse and ordered a burger. Her explanation would have to wait, as would Shelly's, who wrote: **What'd you find out? Did you see that coward Jim on TV running from reporters? Did he ever call you back?**

I badly wanted to tell Shelly that I'd found Savannah and was convinced that she was having an affair with Jim. But I could be wrong and set her off telling everyone, including Mimi Maxwell.

Still in KY but no word from Jim, I wrote back.

Just as my food arrived, so did a text.

Hey lady where r u?

It was from Joey.

In Danville about to stuff my face. Call you in 20?

Where? I drove by that address but didn't see your car.

You're here? I texted.

Yes, where are u now?

Picking up food at this place called Cattleman's Roadhouse.

Just passed it. Don't move. See you in a minute.

Joey was the only person I *did* want to talk to. The only one who might be able to make heads or tails out of what I'd learned and what it could mean. The restaurant was nearly empty on a Monday at rush hour, so I grabbed my takeout and sat in a booth by the window. Not too long after, Joey was sliding in on the other side.

"Hello, Miss Manning," he said, casually, in contrast to the current circumstance.

"What are you doing here?" I asked preemptively.

"Making sure you stay out of trouble . . . and safe."

"You drove all the way here? Are you kidding me? That's over six hours."

"Who are you telling? I know. That's how crazy you've made me," he said. "Believe me, I almost turned around—a couple of times. But that was before you sent me that picture of a house. You were supposed to follow up. I didn't know what to think."

His exasperation was warranted. I had no excuse but was charmed by the lengths he had gone to have my back.

"I'm sorry about that, Joe. I crashed when I got to my room. I was exhausted. I'm really glad you're here, though. I found Savannah. I talked to her."

"What?!"

"Yeah. Her and her husband, Sterling."

"By yourself?"

"Just listen to me for a minute. Okay?"

"Fine." Joey sat back and grabbed a complimentary dinner roll from a basket on the table.

"After I got here today, I was staking out the house when I got a huge break. I overheard them having a pretty vicious argument. It was a screaming match. Sterling said something like, 'This is your fault. I'm in this situation because of you.' And she yelled back: 'You couldn't take care of us.' I think they're having financial problems. But get this . . . she's pregnant, but her husband doesn't know."

"How in the—"

"But wait," I interrupted, and leaned in like someone was spying on us. "That's not the most shocking part. Savannah has been soliciting men for sex on a gaming site. Justin did some digging for me and sent me a picture of her posing like a model in a triple-X magazine. He said one of his friends told him she offered to have sex with him for four hundred dollars. In Indianapolis! Joey, that's where Victoria said Savannah had been visiting family before she came by her house. I think she's been doing this to make ends meet. And I have a theory. That's how she met Jim."

"He's the number one suspect. You know that, right?" Joey asked.

"I have no doubt. But she was pretending to be Marla's

friend and then ended up using her debit card. You know, I kept thinking, who stops to buy lingerie when they could be suspected of murder? But now it makes sense."

"So, together, Jim and Savannah set Marla up . . ." Joey said.

"Then went in for the kill," I said, completing the thought.

Joey sighed. "Wow, this is incredible. Jordan, how do you know she's pregnant?"

"I followed her today. She went to see her doctor for her three-month checkup. Later, when I went to talk to Sterling, I let it slip that he was about to be a father soon, trying to get him to open up. He didn't know anything about the pregnancy."

Joey huffed. "She didn't tell him because it ain't his."

"Well, exactly. She came home shortly after I got there, and you should've seen her face when she saw me."

"What do you mean?"

"She recognized me from the doctor's office."

Joey leaned his back against the bench and pressed his hands over his eyes and forehead. Only his mouth visible. His nostrils flared as he took a deep breath to regulate his reaction.

"Jordan, you're doing way too much. That's why I'm here."

The genuine concern in his eyes incited feelings of guilt in me but only momentarily.

"I'm not finished. Sterling knows about the affair. When they were arguing, he accused her of meeting him—he didn't say a name, just *him*—and implied that Marla caught them at it."

"If she's soliciting, maybe she blamed it on an affair to cover it up."

"Could be," I said.

"Okay, okay, back up," he said. "I remember you telling me that Savannah and Marla were friends."

"She even let Marla borrow her car."

"While sleeping with her husband?" Joey asked.

I nodded.

"And Savannah's husband knows about the affair but probably doesn't know that she's soliciting," he said.

"He's a different kind of man if he does, I'll say that. Savannah did say during their fight, 'What kind of man does that make you?' I'm not saying he doesn't have a job, but he was at home in the middle of the day."

"You know I can't ignore this information, right?" Joey said.

"I thought you said it's technically not your case," I reminded him in a sarcastic tone. "What I don't get is why haven't the local police brought Savannah in yet for questioning. Don't they have enough evidence by now, with departments in three states working on this?"

"They don't know what you know about her," he said. "What they have is circumstantial."

"That's nuts to me."

What was our next move? Even after going over everything we both knew, Joey and I were struggling to come up with a game plan. There were still too many unknowns.

34

Marla was last seen dropping off her kids at school. She had a job interview and an appointment to see an apartment that day but didn't show up for either one. What happened to the car?

Joey told me that there were alerts on the license plate coast to coast. "If that car was on the road anywhere, it would have been spotted by now," he said.

After I got back to the hotel, the argument between Savannah and Sterling played over and over in my head. She'd shouted, *You weren't even supposed to be there!* He'd responded, You're the reason I'm in this situation. It was late. I was wide awake and thought about calling Joey, who followed me back to the Super 8 and insisted on renting the room next door. Admittedly, having him close by did provide an extra layer of comfort.

I pulled out my laptop and searched "lodging in Kentland, Indiana." Victoria had mentioned that Savannah said she was staying at a motor inn. Was Jim there, too? Is that why he popped up in Rensselaer so soon after Marla disappeared? Was Sterling there? When did he learn of the affair? Was he trying to catch her in the act?

Kentland was a half-hour drive from Rensselaer, with about a third of the population. It wasn't exactly a tourist spot. There were no major hotel chains and only one motel, the Birchwood, a one-story throwback to the 1970s that offered single, double, or king beds, and rooms with a kitchen for a steep upcharge.

I closed my laptop and called up an unanswered text Nate had sent earlier. **Hello beautiful. How's your day?** Nate might be the distraction I needed at the moment, a brain reset to help me step back and assess all the information that had been coming at me today.

> **It's been hectic. I'm in Kentucky following a lead in a murder case.**

Delete.

Sadly, I wasn't sure how to draft a response that didn't make me sound like a vigilante. I called instead.

"Well, if it isn't the lovely Jordan Manning," Nate said. "How are you today?"

"I'm good. Sorry I didn't get back to you earlier. I'm out of town on a story."

"Oh, really? That sounds exciting. Where?"

"Don't be jealous," I teased. "Danville, Kentucky. I had dinner at the nicest restaurant in town, and it had *cattle* in the name."

"Ha! That's funny. You're cute. When are you coming back? I don't know what you did to me, but I'm starting to miss you."

That was the nicest thing Nate Fisher had ever said to me and his most forward play for my heart yet. I wanted very much to return that energy, to free my mind from Savannah's troubled marriage and crazy lifestyle and the mysterious disappearance of Marla Hancock, when another call came in.

"That's sweet," I managed to say before excusing myself. "Nate, I've got a call coming in. Can you give me a minute to see who this is? I'll be right back."

"Sure."

"Hello? This is Jordan Manning."

"This is Savannah Moultrie."

Oh shit! Are you kidding me? The heat must be on. It's starting to sink in how much trouble she is in. If that was her on the ATM video trying to use Marla's card, that's a felony. She's three months pregnant, and from the looks of it, it's not her husband's child. If one or both of these things are true, oh man!

"You have no idea the hell you've put me in," she said, projecting blame. "Why didn't you just come to me?"

The hell I put her in?

"I did come to you, Savannah, and I have a lot of questions. The first being, what happened to Marla?"

"I don't know where Marla is."

"So she just left her kids, took off in *your* car, and what? Went into hiding?"

"Yes, she did take off in the car I'm still paying the insurance on. I'm ticked off, but I'm also worried about her."

"You tried to use her debit card."

"No, I didn't. That was Marla. But her husband apparently cut her off financially and it didn't work."

Savannah must have felt certain that her emphatic denial exonerated her. I lowered the boom.

"How do you explain the lingerie store? You came back the next day and placed the same order that had been in Marla's name a day before and paid cash."

But Savannah wouldn't be backed into a corner. She was a lot tougher than even I'd thought.

"Like I said, she tried to use the card because her husband lied and told her there was money back in the account. I always got the feeling that Marla was living a double life. She didn't share it with me, and her husband certainly didn't know what was going on."

Savannah had gotten good at playing this game against less worthy opponents. But her confidence was starting to erode, and she sounded nervous and breathy. She was all over the place. I could only imagine what shape she was in.

"Why did the lingerie go to your house and not to where Marla was staying?" I asked.

"Because she was buying it for me as a thank-you for letting her use the car. That's the last time I saw her. I really liked the pieces, so I went back the next day and bought them myself."

If she's making this up, she's a damn good liar. Even I have to admit, that's a plausible explanation.

"Was Jim with you?" I asked.

"What?"

"Are you two having an affair?"

"Jim has nothing to do with this! He hadn't seen Marla in months!"

By defending Jim, Savannah was exposed. And, before she realized she had been checked in this game of chess, I pressed on.

"But you don't deny the affair?"

The other end of the receiver was so quiet, I expected to soon hear the frantic sounds of a busy signal any moment.

"Jim asked me to keep an eye on Marla to see if he could get any dirt on her."

Finally, a morsel of truth.

"So, you were sleeping with Jim," I stated as fact. "And you tricked Marla into thinking you were her friend?"

"That's not a crime."

No, but it's dirty.

"You're right, it's not. But it does place you and Jim under suspicion. He's the main suspect."

"I'm telling you; Jimmy didn't have anything to do with this!"

There it was. Jimmy. The affectionate nickname Marla called her husband that made Shelly gag every time she heard it.

"Marla isn't blameless in this, you know. I think she's playing us both. Maybe she found out about us. Maybe she was upset—understandably—and went off somewhere to deal with it, and maybe somebody else got to her. I don't know. But it wasn't Jim!"

"You were staying in Kentland, right?"

"Where'd you hear that?"

"Victoria. Marla's best friend, whom you met. You remember? She told me she overheard the two of you talking. Was Jim with you?"

"No-o-o!" she said emphatically.

"Was Sterling?"

"No."

"Where'd you stay?"

"What difference does it make?"

Savannah fought to regain her composure. The fact that she didn't want to tell me led me to believe it made a huge difference.

"Are you in love with him?"

"I was, but it's over. It's too complicated now. You can judge us all you want, but Marla's fate was of her own choosing. I talked to Jim every day when I was in Indiana and Chicago. Often from his office line. He wasn't anywhere close to Marla."

Savannah seemed more concerned about exonerating Jim than protecting her own skin. Didn't she realize that her actions made her a suspect, too?

"Then go on the air with me and say that. Clear him. It would be a taped interview. We can do it right here in Danville."

"Only if it's okay with Jim."

Shelly confronted her sister for falling back into victim mode and letting Jim call the shots. And now Savannah was deferring to his judgment. If I were creating a profile on Jim, *narcissistic* and *manipulative* would be two words I would use to describe him.

"Let me know by tomorrow. You may be sure Jim is innocent, but the authorities are far from that."

It was only after we hung up that I remembered putting Nate on hold, but he was already gone.

Sorry, my call went long. Something's come up. I'll call you tomorrow, I texted, then called Joey.

"Hey, Joey. I hope I didn't wake you."

"No, what's up?"

"Savannah just called."

"Really? What'd she say?"

"She agreed to do an interview if Jim says it's okay. I gave her a deadline, though. Tomorrow. I'm going to drive back to Indiana in the morning, see if I can't get some answers at the motel in Kentland where she might have been staying."

"What do you think you'll find?"

"When I asked, Savannah wouldn't tell me the name of the motel. Considering everything else she's admitted to, that seems strange."

"You're right, it does," Joey said. "It's an unnecessary omission. If she called you after what happened today, then she's desperate. And that's when criminals slip up. You can't surveil them now that they've seen you. But I can. Go do your thing in Indiana. I'll keep an eye on Savannah and Sterling."

35

Now wide awake but fatigued, all I could think about was lying down in cool sheets and resting my head. I got undressed and slid beneath the covers. I turned on the television and lowered the volume to barely above a hum and hoped the muffled sound would lull me to sleep. It worked, because a few hours later, I was jolted awake by a ceaseless dull ringing sound. The station was running a test of the emergency broadcast system. The digital clock's giant red numbers showed 2:32 A.M. I felt my way through the dark to the bathroom. The light over the mirror flickered on and off before settling on a blinding white glow. Then suddenly a thought occurred to me: *News trucks won't still be parked outside Jim's house at this hour, will they?*

Jim Hancock must feel like a prisoner in his own home. That is, if he hadn't managed to sneak away and move to another location to escape the media swarm for a second day. Or could he be hunkered down waiting for an opportunity to bolt to a worksite in the morning or to his parents' house? Would Jim and Savannah risk meeting out somewhere?

I got dressed, grabbed my coat and purse, and took the back stairs two floors down to the parking lot. Outside everything was quiet. The cold, dewy air blew tiny drops of water that stuck to the windshield like ice. I got in my car and typed into the GPS the address Shelly had texted me.

I sat there for a moment with the engine running before backing out of the motel parking lot into the ghost town that was Danville at a quarter to three in the morning. The streets were empty, but I of course caught every other red light on the outer drive before merging onto the freeway in the opposite direction from Savannah's place. The landscape brightened with each exit I passed, revealing the beautiful vistas I'd driven by on my way into town. Jim's subdivision was a stark contrast to the Moultries', with sizable luxurious brick homes on large plots of land surrounded by lush green lawns and long circular drives. The Hancock home was made of a beige brick and stood two stories high, with large triple-pane windows and regal brass light sconces flanking a beautifully lacquered dark blue door. The long driveway curved around the side of the house to a three-car garage divided into two and one. A house like this in Courtney's wealthy suburb north of Chicago would go for a million dollars easily. Here, a homeowner could score a find like this for maybe half that price but still gain the same level of prestige.

It must have been pretty bad for Marla to leave all this behind. But this would be a major come-up for Savannah.

I parked farther down the block but still felt too exposed. After the frenzied media scene earlier today, I wouldn't be surprised if a neighbor spotted an out-of-the-ordinary car and called the police. I looked suspicious sitting in my car in the middle of the night. There weren't any mature trees to provide cover. They all had skinny trunks, and of course it was too early in the season for leaves. You can tell how old a neighborhood is by its trees. These homes were new construction, which made sense, since Jim was a contractor who quite possibly had this house built himself. At least from this vantage point, I could see the garage and front door, but there could be a back door out of sight that he could use to exit.

My nervousness left me queasy. I opened the glove box stocked with snacks and mints and grabbed two peppermints, hoping to lessen the sensation. Three o'clock. Three-fifteen. Three-thirty. I was grateful no one had called the cops to check out the Black woman just sitting in her car and thought about quitting while I was ahead. Just when I started feeling silly, a light came from the porch.

Oh crap!

The front door opened and a barefooted man wearing jogging pants and a V-neck tee stepped out onto the porch. The porch lights illuminated his face and thinning hair. He was not fit. In fact, his stomach looked a little round, like a ball was tucked beneath his shirt. He looked nothing like I'd imagined he would. He wasn't intimidating or threatening in any way. He was just an average Joe—or in this case, Jim. After all I'd heard about him from Shelly and Victoria, I couldn't believe I was now yards from this guy.

Where's he going?

He nervously searched his surroundings. I saw his attention shift to the mailbox at the end of the driveway. With no news vans or reporters at his front door, he likely saw this as an opening to grab the mail, probably the first time since his name made front-page news. He sighed, then moved back into the house.

I got out of the car and walked toward the front door.

Am I really about to do this? It's not too late to change your mind.

I knocked on the door. Seconds later, the porch went pitch-dark and I heard the click of the dead bolt. I was terrified. I knew what I wanted to say and wouldn't have long to get it out.

"Finally! What took . . ." Jim started to say.

"Expecting Savannah?" I blurted out.

Jim glared into my eyes. His expression quickly morphed into a disgusted sneer. "Who the fuck are you? Coming to my house at this hour?"

"Jordan Manning. I'm a TV reporter from Chicago," I said matter-of-factly, as if we'd run into each other in the grocery store.

"A reporter? You mean I've had to put up with you people all day and now you're knocking on my door at four o'clock in the morning?"

"That's what reporters do, Jim. We knock on doors," I said.

He let out an uncomfortable sigh. "Oh yeah. I remember you now. I got your message."

"I've called you several times, Jim," I said, getting back to the topic at hand. "I've spoken to Savannah. Just a few hours ago, in fact."

I stopped talking to let that sink in. It still wasn't too late for Jim to slam the door in my face. But the fact that he hadn't already let me know that dropping the Savannah bomb was smart and gave me some leverage.

"Look, as far as I know, you're not a suspect. But you and I both know that police might look at you differently if they found out about the affair. They might already know. And not only about the affair, but you were having your mistress follow your wife? Do you know how that looks?"

Jim's body shifted and he stared at the ground. "What do you want from me?"

"I want you to go on air and tell your side of the story. If you had nothing to do with Marla's disappearance . . ."

"You know, the cops aren't even saying she disappeared," he said.

"Why? Because you led them to believe that she left and now she's hiding? Hiding from who? You?"

"I led them to believe Marla's hiding? Are you insane?"

He shook his head and his arms rose and collapsed at his sides. "I'm just so tired of this! Marla left me. Okay? Yes, I've made some mistakes, but she didn't even want the kids!"

"I heard neither did you," I said. "How do you feel about having another one on the way?"

Those words landed like a punch. Jim took a deep breath and opened the door wider, gesturing toward the living room. "Look, why don't you come in and let's sit down and talk about this?"

"I'm fine right here. Thank you."

He massaged his prominent forehead lines and ran his hand across his scalp.

"You have my number," I said. "Will you think about it?"

He sighed. "I . . . I probably should be thanking you," he said. "This is hard."

I squared my shoulders and folded my arms. My face tightened in an expression of utter disbelief.

"I'm sure it is. But why should you be thanking me?" I asked.

"Look, I don't know where Marla is, but wherever she is, good or bad, I had nothing to do with it or with her."

"Then what do you have to lose?"

"I know it looks bad, okay? It's not just me I'm thinking about. It's my family's business. My mom and dad, their reputation. My kids. We're gonna want to sit down and talk . . . at some point. I just can't say when right now. I don't know who to trust. I need to figure that out first."

Either Jim Hancock wasn't the intimidating bully Shelly made him out to be or he was masterful at wiggling out of situations.

"Okay," I said. "That's fair."

36

Tuesday, March 24

Savannah told her husband she'd broken off the affair. When we spoke, what I heard in her voice was a woman in love now panicking at the thought of losing him. After seeing Jim and how he lived, I was beginning to wonder whether it was social status and financial gain that made Savannah fall in love with Jim. *Didn't Shelly say she believed that was what attracted her sister, too?*

The sun was dawning by the time I got back to the hotel and gathered my things. Before I got on the road, I searched online and downloaded images of Marla and Sterling. I found one of Jim with the kids when they were really small from Marla's Facebook page. Marla, like moms so often do, likely took that picture of Jim, and that's why she wasn't in it.

The Birchwood Motor Inn looked even more dilapidated up close than it did online. More of a motel hell occupying its own island of concrete and patchy grass in the middle of nowhere. A plaid living room chair partially blocked the office door, which triggered an alert, a buzzing sound, when I opened it. The room inside was cramped, with a faux marble reception desk, a window air-conditioning unit, and a mini fridge with a microwave on top. Room keys with color-coded tags were fully exposed on a corkboard behind the desk. Not the most secure setup.

A gentleman who looked to be in his mid to late sixties emerged from the back and took his place behind the desk. "Good day. How can I help you?"

"Hi, my name is Jordan Manning. I'm with News Channel 8 in Chicago." I laid my work badge and a business card on the counter.

"Dad, are you up front?" said a voice from the back.

The gentleman turned his head and looked over his left shoulder. "Yes, Jewel! I've got it! Pardon me. Now, what were you saying, young lady?"

"I'm doing a story on a young mother from Rensselaer who vanished about a month ago. I believe she might have been with a woman who stayed here."

I pulled out my phone and showed him a picture of Marla. "Do you recognize her?" He reached for my phone, but I wouldn't let it go and moved it closer to him. "Well, I can't hardly see that there on your phone. Can you make it bigger?"

"I'm sorry, but no, not really. Here." I pushed the image closer to his face and he leaned in, squinting.

"My eyes aren't so good, but I can't say that I recall seeing this person," he said.

"Do you check in most of your guests? Or does Jewel, who you were just talking to?"

"We share the load. But I'm pretty sure she can see that there on your phone better than I can. Jewel!" he yelled over his shoulder again.

"What?"

"Can you come up here for a minute?"

A young woman emerged from the back. She was almost a dead ringer for the actress Courteney Cox, except for the silver swath of hair across the top of her head and a dimple in her chin that she clearly inherited from her father.

"What can I do for you?" she asked.

"This lady here is with the television news in Chicago," her father said.

"Hi, I'm Jordan Manning." I held out my phone and showed her the picture of Marla. "Do you recognize this woman?"

"I can't say that I do," she said.

Next, I pulled up the picture of Savannah that Justin had sent me, placing my thumb over the bottom half. "What about her?"

"Yeah, I remember her," Jewel said without hesitation. "She was acting real strange."

"Strange how?" I asked.

"She stayed over an extra night and tried to cut a deal with me. She got mad when I wouldn't agree to it. I figure that's why she took everything she could carry out of that room with her. The shower curtain, the towels, the bedspread, even the sheets."

"Was she alone?"

"I don't remember seeing anyone with her when she checked in. Do you, Daddy?"

The older man shrugged his shoulders.

"Her name's Savannah Moultrie. Do you remember what room she was staying in?" I asked.

"I can look it up," Jewel said. "How do you spell her last name?"

"M-o-u-l-t-r-i-e."

"Hold on. I remember that name. There's a town in Georgia called Moultrie," her father said. "She wasn't alone. Her husband joined her, remember, Jewel? She left a key at the desk," he said, proving useful after all.

"Found her!" Jewel said. "She was here for several nights."

"When?" I asked.

"She checked in February 21."

I showed them both Jim's picture. "Do either of you recognize this man?"

"I don't see all too well. I'm sorry," Jewel's father reminded me.

"Jewel?"

"No."

"What room was she in?" I asked.

"One eleven."

"Is that room empty now?"

"Yes, it is. We're not too busy this time of year."

"Do you mind showing it to me?"

"You said you're a reporter, not the cops, right?" Jewel asked.

"Yes. Jewel, this is literally a matter of life-or-death."

She pulled out a cell phone and texted someone. "Let me go get the master key."

Jewel led me around to the building all the way to the back of the property. The motel was made up of four low-slung buildings separated by a parking lot with a dedicated space outside each room. Room 111 was sparsely furnished with a queen-size bed, a nightstand, a window air conditioner, and a mini fridge/microwave setup like the one in the office.

"Excuse me. I'll be right back."

I ran to my car and grabbed my emergency preparedness bag—my friends call it my "bug-out bag"—and a fresh pair of latex gloves.

"I don't know what you hope to find. It's been a while and we do a thorough job of cleaning," Jewel said.

I felt around the back of the nightstand drawer that had a Gideon Bible and a bunch of menus from local diners and fast-food delivery spots. "Can you help me pull the bed out from the wall? I want to look behind there."

Jewel and I posted up on either side of the headboard and scooted the bed a couple of feet from the wall. "Knock-knock," said a man at the door.

"Can you help us pull this bed back, Darnell?" Jewel asked.

I hadn't expected to see anyone who looked like me in Kentland. But there he was, a fraction of the 1.68 percent of African Americans who lived here.

"Did you lose something, ma'am?" he asked me.

"She's a reporter from Chicago looking into a missing person case," Jewel said.

I knelt on the floor and closely examined the carpet for something, anything, that might have gotten stuck in there. The bed frame was old and worn. I pulled a flashlight from my purse and lay on my back to inspect beneath the bed. But it was still too dark.

"I need to flip the bed over so I can get a better look. But here, just a sec," I said, reaching into my bug-out bag and pulling out a spare pair of latex gloves. "Can you put these on first?"

"Sure," he said, squeezing his large hands into the medium-size gloves.

Darnell squatted like he was competing for the title of the world's strongest man and tilted the bed up to expose its underside, resting it against the wall.

"How old is this frame? Any idea?"

"That frame is probably older than me," Darnell said.

"Yeah, but we reinforce the sides with plywood to keep folks from bending them up. People are hard on these beds," said Jewel.

"Show me."

Darnell peeled back the mattress, revealing a strip of plywood, pristine except for deep ruby, blackish streaks about four or five inches long. I lifted the wood up off the frame. Whatever made the stain had to be liquid because it continued on the underside, but the color was slightly different. More of a brownish red color. With less exposure to the air, the oxidation process wasn't as transformational.

"This is blood." I stood up and backed away from the bed. "This room is a potential crime scene."

"Blood? How do you know for sure?" Jewel asked.

"I've studied forensics. I'm sure."

Darnell moved toward the bed. "I'll put this back."

"No!" I said, waving my arms. "Leave it. Don't touch anything else."

Next to the bed was a nightstand made of solid wood, not that prefab material so often used by discount furniture makers. The top was covered with a piece of beveled glass that was chipped on the corner. I tapped my gloved hand on the glass. It was sharp.

"We should get out of here. I'm calling the police."

Instead of dialing 911, I called Joey.

"Hey, Jordie, what's up?"

"Joey, I found bloodstains on a bed frame at a hotel in Kentland where Savannah and I believe her husband, too, were staying a little over a month ago."

"You call the local police?"

"No, but I'm calling you. Look, I don't want to have to explain to the locals what I'm doing here. You're on the task force; you can get the state police here quicker than I can."

"Good point. I'm on it," he said.

"Okay, thanks."

I turned around to a flabbergasted-looking Jewel and Darnell and again pulled up the picture of Jim on my phone. "Are you sure you don't recognize this man?"

They both studied the image. "Sorry, he doesn't look familiar," Jewel said.

"The guy who was staying here kind of reminded me of this actor on one of those legal shows," Darnell said. "He looked stressed out."

I pulled up the picture of Sterling. "Is this him?"

"Yeah, I believe it is," Darnell said.

"Oh my god, he does kind of look like that actor. I forget the name of the show," Jewel said.

"Darnell, what makes you so sure this is the guy?" I asked.

"I remember he had a deep crease in his forehead. You can see it there in the picture."

He was right. It was a distinguishable characteristic.

"I remember something else," he continued. "I was making rounds with the supplies cart, and he caught up and asked me for a Do Not Disturb sign and extra towels. And he was adamant they didn't want the room cleaned until they left."

A memory flooded my mind. *The public defender at the Morales hearing.* His aggressive action toward her caused her to stumble backward and nearly hit her head on the sharp corner of the prosecutor's table. For that, Morales was additionally charged with second-degree assault. She went down hard and fast. With that kind of momentum, she came within an inch of permanent brain damage or losing her life. Is that what happened to Marla? The edge of that nightstand was sharp as a blade. Was it weaponized? There was only one conclusion. They were cleaning up a murder.

37

Wednesday, March 25

Ellen helped arrange the taped interview with Savannah, a national exclusive, at our local affiliate station. The lighting at the Channel 17 studios in Danville was harsh and fluorescent. The building was dated. But the location didn't matter. It was the storytelling that people cared about. The setting of the interview was inside a conference room, not in the studio itself. Two chairs were set up across from each other, with lights positioned on both sides. It's remarkable how much a television interview set could resemble an interrogation room in a police precinct.

"You'd better bring it, Jordan," Ellen said. "We're all counting on you."

Ellen was my friend and cheerleader, but she had some skin in this game, too. So did Joey. He alerted the Indiana state police based on a "tip" he got about what appeared to be blood at the Birchwood motel room.

"They've sealed off the room and sent in a forensic specialist to collect the blood sample for analysis," he said. "Another forensic specialist."

I could feel Joey smiling through the phone.

We wouldn't know anything conclusive, though, overnight. There remained the gut-wrenching ask of Marla's family and

Jim, technically still her husband, to sign off on the release of medical records that could help the science either prove or disprove the blood was hers.

"Are we ready yet?" I asked impatiently, anxious to get the interview rolling before Savannah changed her mind. She'd called the night before to tell me that "Jim thinks I should do the interview." Though he declined to join her. So much for "we" are going to want to talk about it, just not yet.

I was headed back to Rensselaer, but I skipped the stopover and drove straight back to Danville, where Savannah was now staying with her sister. The irony. She felt forced to flee her house on Manassas Lane to escape Sterling's relentless questioning about her affair and other secrets. Now, a few feet away, sitting tall in her seat, back arched and her hands primly folded in her lap like a debutante, she was here not so much for herself as for Jim. That image would soon be shattered.

"Savannah, how long have you been friends with Marla Hancock?"

"Not for long. Maybe half a year."

"What's she like?"

She shrugged. "I don't know. She's nice. Normal. Marla has a hard time seeing what's right in front of her."

"How would you describe your relationship with Jim Hancock, Marla's husband?"

"They were estranged."

"What does that have to do with your relationship with Jim?"

"I met Jim in the chat room for World of Warcraft. It's a popular video game. We decided to meet up and started seeing each other pretty regularly."

"But you saw other men, too? Isn't that right?"

She hesitated. "I'm not sure what you mean."

"Yes you do. I obtained an image of you posing in some really racy lingerie. You sent that image to a player on a streaming site."

Savannah's gaze was intense, but she didn't respond.

"And you're also married?"

"Yes, but I came clean. My husband knows about the affair."

"Did Marla know?"

"She suspected Jim was involved with someone but . . ."

"She had no idea it was you?"

She shook her head.

"And now you're pregnant. Is it Jim's?"

Savannah nodded.

"So here's the big question I have for you, Savannah. Why did you befriend Marla while you were sleeping with her husband?"

Savannah's bottled-up anxiety exploded into tears. She pressed her hands against her cheeks. "I need a moment," she said, and one of the producers reached in and handed her a box of tissues.

I pressed on. "You even let her borrow your car and dropped in on her in Rensselaer. That's very suspicious behavior."

She dabbed at her tears. "Jim asked me to keep an eye on her."

"Jim did?"

"She'd been to drug rehab a year earlier. She got hooked on antidepressants and he said she was drinking a lot. He was worried about the kids."

"Are you saying that Jim sent you to spy on his wife?"

Another question Savannah debated with herself whether to answer. I could see in her expression, in the way her eyes searched the room, that she was wrestling with her moral compass, running from the truth that was chasing her. I remained silent. It's an art form. A lot of reporters try to fill that dead air, but I've learned that within that sustained silence, people—even the worst ones—can be tougher on themselves than I ever needed to be.

"When Jim wrote in a private message to you 'I thought you wanted to play for keeps,' how did you interpret that?"

Savannah looked like she'd seen a ghost, clearly unaware that Shelly had gotten her hands on an image of the chat messages between her and Jim. "We wanted to be together. But a divorce from Marla wasn't going to come cheap. She didn't have a job or any skills."

"Not like you, huh?"

Savannah fidgeted with the drawstring at the waist of her dress. Her confidence was shrinking.

"What do you mean?" she asked.

"I was made aware of something very personal about you, Savannah. Your online activities didn't end with Jim. Did they? There were others."

Savannah collapsed into tears.

"I know this is difficult, but I need you to hear me," I said. "There was blood found in your motel room in Kentland, Indiana. Was Jim with you at any time during your stay?"

"No! No! No! It wasn't Jim! It was Sterling! He followed me there thinking he'd catch us, but he got Marla instead."

Savannah bent over and buried her face in her hands. Now I was the one under threat of losing my composure. "What do you mean, he got Marla?"

"Sterling broke into my gaming account and got an address Jim gave me in Rensselaer. He thought we were going to meet up there, but it was actually where Marla was staying. He followed me to the motel. He was waiting for Jim to show up. Jim was never coming. Marla was in the room waiting for me to come back with food when Sterling somehow got the room key and barged in on her. He was in a rage, asking, 'Where's Jim?'"

"You were there for this?"

"No, he told me about it later. When I came back, Marla was on the floor."

"What did he say happened?" I asked.

"Sterling said they were at each other's throats, arguing back and forth."

"What would they have to argue about?"

"He was trying to convince her that I wasn't her friend. Marla didn't believe him. She said she was going to call me and went to grab her phone out of her bag and he pushed her, and she fell backward and hit her head on the nightstand."

I could see the artery alongside her neck pulsing.

"I've asked you this before, Savannah, and I'll ask you again. Is Marla dead?"

She nodded with an anguished, distraught look on her face. "It was an accident! It was an accident!" Repeating the words several times, she then finally added more to the story, telling me, "The corner of the nightstand was sharp. Sterling told me her head hit it. She fell to the ground and never opened her eyes. He thought she was unconscious."

I felt as if the room was spinning out of control. Savannah was now a blurry figure in front of me, and I could feel my own pulse frantically beating. *How could Savannah hold onto this story? I'm confused. Was this an accident? Is she lying again?* I felt a rush of sadness at the thought that those poor children would soon learn their mother had been killed.

"Where's Marla's body?" I asked.

"I don't know. Only Sterling knows that. I told him I didn't want to know."

Savannah went on sobbing. Around the room, jaws dropped en masse.

Savannah's sister, who'd accompanied her to the interview, rushed over to comfort her, something Shelly would never have the chance to do again for Marla.

There were knots in my stomach. I didn't even remember walking away. The next thing I recalled was hearing my own voice speaking into my cell phone: "I'd like to report a murder."

38

Thursday, March 26

Diana Sorano: We start off with a shocking and bizarre conclusion to the heartbreaking story of a missing Indiana mom. Police have charged the husband of a woman who now admits to having had an affair with the missing woman's husband. Jordan Manning joins us in the studio with her exclusive interview with that woman, which helped solve this tragic case.

There I was, on set with Diana and Simone Michele four days after I was supposed to fill in for the morning anchor, still on the desk, in the big chair, though not in the way I could ever have imagined.

The station started hyping the big exclusive while I was still in the air. Ellen was on pins and needles hoping I would make my flight to Chicago in time for the broadcast at five. Justice Jordan would live up to the name.

Channel 17 fed my interview with Savannah to the station to ramp up the scoop while a copy was turned over to the authorities, who launched a manhunt for Sterling Moultrie. It was brief. He was in custody by the time I landed at O'Hare.

They got him! Joey related in a text I received just as I was taxiing to the gate.

Joey's surveillance proved helpful. After Savannah named Sterling as Marla's killer, I called 911. Joey then picked things up from there, tailing Sterling to Lexington, about forty-five minutes away, and tipping the police off as to where they could find him. Joey was told he confessed in the back of the squad car before they could make it to the station and told them where they could find Marla's body.

Ellen sent a car to pick me up at the airport and ferry me directly to the station. I was in and out of hair and makeup in time to sit at the anchor desk for the opening credits of the five o'clock news.

Jordan: Thank you, Diana and Simone. There are so many twists and turns in this complicated love triangle that, literally, led me to the doorstep of the man accused of killing Marla Hancock. Police arrested Sterling Moultrie outside the airport in Lexington, Kentucky. He confessed to the murder and told the police where he buried Marla's body. Just hours before his arrest, I sat down for this exclusive interview with his wife, Savannah Moultrie, who revealed what she says happened to Marla, who was last seen almost a month ago.

After the nearly two-minute segment ran, both Diana and Simone were left glaring at the monitors placed discreetly on the news desk. Simone gathered her composure to blurt out the question likely being asked by viewers at home.

Simone Michele: What led you to Savannah and Sterling?

Jordan: It may be hard for people to wrap their minds around this. It's 2009. The internet is becoming a dark world used for all kinds of things. In this case, you have a couple who was financially strapped and concocted a plan to meet people on a gaming system. The plan was to trade sex for money. Sources tell me people make thousands of dollars doing this. Imagine what it will be like in ten or fifteen years.

Back to you, Simone and Diana.

A lot of times anchors don't do follow-ups. But the shock of it all led Diana to ask, "What's happening with Marla's husband?"

Jordan: Authorities say Jim Hancock had nothing to do with Marla's death and won't be charged. As for Savannah, they say she's cooperating.

I couldn't share everything I knew with the viewers without betraying Joey's trust. That morning, he shared with me what Savannah had told police during their interrogation.

"Joe, I'm still not convinced that Savannah and Jim weren't planning to take care of the Marla problem. Are you?"

"We might never know the truth," he said. "But I don't buy her reason for spying on Marla, either."

"What'd she say?"

"That she was trying to catch Marla relapsing on pills or booze to help Jim in the custody battle. That's not for public consumption. Got it?"

"I've got you."

After the broadcast, Ellen was waiting for me off the set.

"Ugh! I don't know whether to shake you or hug you," she said, sighing heavily. "Come here."

"Should I be worried?"

"Get over here!" Ellen opted for the hug instead. "I'm so angry with you, but relieved that you're safe. Great work!"

"Thanks for hanging in there with me, Ellen."

"Drinks tonight?" she asked.

"Rain check? I'm tired. I'm going to catch up on emails and go home. And you need to figure out how to get my car back to Chicago."

"Maybe I'll just fly you back there and you can drive it home," she said.

"You wouldn't."

Ellen smirked and walked away. "Ellen? Ellen!" This was one time I didn't appreciate sustained silence.

39

Not ready to talk about the last few days, preferring that the story that just aired speak for me, I made a beeline for my cubicle-walled desk. I felt numb and truly drained. Up until now, this had been an out-of-body experience. But off the air, it all became real. Marla wouldn't be going home, her children would learn the awful truth about what happened to their mother, and Jim would live in her shadow. I decided to wait until morning to call and check on Shelly and see how Marla's kids were doing. It's always a struggle, the relationship as a journalist that I'm supposed to have after the story is over.

"They don't know yet," Shelly told me when I spoke to her the next day. "I begged Jim not to tell them until I get there. I'm driving out there tomorrow morning."

"And he agreed?"

"Yeah. It's the most decent thing he's ever done," she said. "Still, if he hadn't been fooling around with that skank, my sister would still be alive."

I couldn't blame her for not seeing it any other way and hoped another crime wasn't about to be committed.

"Jordan, I might have never known what happened to my sister if it hadn't been for you. If I said thank you every day for the rest of my life, it wouldn't be enough."

"Oh, the police would have figured it out eventually," I said humbly.

"Humph! Maybe, maybe not."

"You take care, Shelly. And don't let Jim keep those kids from you. They need you."

As I headed for my desk, Jenny B. was standing near my cubicle, her brows lifted, nodding approval.

"Hey, Jenny. What are you doing here?"

"When I heard about the interview with that woman, I needed to come in and say, 'Great work!' in person, Jordan."

"Thank you, Jenny. You were there from day one. You took that first call."

That's the complicated part about this industry. It's competitive, but when we do it right, it's a reminder of how important this work is—and why anchoring, for now, could wait.

My email was packed with unread messages with subject lines marked *Urgent.* "Help, please." "I need you, Jordan." "Important." Finally there it was! The overlooked email from Lisette with an image of an envelope. I clicked on it to open the invitation.

Lisette Holmes and Mike Spencer
Invite you to a Couple's Shower
Saturday, April 11, 2009,
at the Saugatuck Beachfront Inn
RSVP by March 27

Done. Just in time.

I still hadn't friended Lin on Facebook and finally made up my mind I wasn't going to. I decided to end my torment over the man I nearly gave all this up for and let him remain in the past.

Are you free Saturday? I texted Nate.

Running from either version of my life was no longer an option. Justice Jordan Manning, investigative reporter, had a place and a purpose, and just plain old Jordan did, too.

40

Saturday, May 2

The weather was unseasonably warm in Saugatuck, and the usually blustery winds off the shores were calm and I was, too. I arrived two days before the wedding, feeling the need to turn the whole affair into a little mini spa vacation. It was relaxing walking around and taking in the quaint scenery, art galleries, and boutiques along Butler and Griffith Streets. Sipping a glass of pinot grigio on a pier overlooking the lake from Mount Baldhead Park was peaceful, even with the extra layers of clothing needed to stay outside for longer than thirty minutes. I've always been too antsy to fully enjoy a spa day, but this time I was determined to enjoy every moment of the deep tissue massage.

Two days of me time were the perfect windup to the big day. I was ready to play my supporting role to Liz's leading lady and answer the inevitable prying questions about my relationship status. That meant being the charming best friend and the taskmaster all at once. Liz was adamant the rehearsal dinner wrap up before ten o'clock. Her warning to me was clear.

"People will stay until the liquor runs out," she said. "And I'm not in the mood for a long-drawn-out soiree. If one of my pictures has a hint of a dark circle under the eyes, Jordan, I'm blaming you. Just end the night with a toast and tell everyone to get to bed."

I wanted to say, "Lisette, I can't tell adults when to go to bed." Instead of poking the bear, I opted for "Okay, don't worry. I've got this."

My rehearsal dinner toast was brief but, I hoped, still heartfelt. It was challenging to sound sincere with Lisette glaring at me and pointing at the soft flesh beneath her eyes, mouthing "no bags, no dark circles." She reminded me of a floor director ordering me to wrap up my on-set report by twirling a finger in the air. I was sure her gestures didn't go unnoticed. Too bad she couldn't give me the "wrap it up" through an earpiece as an executive producer would when I'm working in the field. In either case, Lisette missed her calling.

"Good evening, can I have your attention?" I said, tapping a knife gently against a champagne glass. By now the bubbly and every other spirit imaginable flowed freely, and the vibration from the chorus of voices talking over one another rose to a roar.

"Hey, guys! Whoo-hoo! Can I have your attention?" I pleaded.

Finally I managed to capture the attention of those at the long rectangular table decorated with stemmed candles and mesmerizing bouquets packed with pink roses and jasmine stems, the bride's favorites.

"It's about time to wrap things up, guys, so I'll be brief. In less than fifteen hours, these two lovebirds are going to become mister and missus."

Cheers and applause erupted in the private dining room of the five-star waterside inn that sat above the dunes.

"However, before we all get the rest needed to make it through tomorrow, I just want to give a toast. And I'm going to try not to get too emotional."

"Oh, Jordan, please don't!" Lisette shouted out with a smirk.

"Lisette, Mike, thank you for sharing your love with us. You are what I've always imagined true love and commitment to be. This is one of those moments you get to have in your life if you're extremely lucky. The chance to celebrate love with the people who have been rooting for it to happen. And, Mike, I just want you to know, I'm not losing a sister, I am gaining a brother. Family. Someone who knows what it's like being bossed around by Lisette."

"You know that's the truth!" Lisette's little sister chimed in, and the room swelled with laughter.

"So please join me in raising your glasses to this stunning pair. Lisette, I love you and cannot wait to watch you dedicate your lives to each other. Cheers!"

Cheers!

"Now, I'm under strict orders to tell you all good night and get some sleep. Tomorrow is going to be a big, fabulous day!"

Perfect. Not too long, not too mushy.

I glanced over at Lisette, who nodded her approval. Turns out my verbal admonishment wasn't enough to get people moving toward the exit, so I had to gently nudge guests to clear the dining room. Afterward, I stopped by the restaurant bar for a nightcap of bourbon with a lemon twist. It was far removed from the lemon drop shots we used to order after the deejay announced last call at the end of a long night at the club, when I was living the dream in my twenties.

"May I take this to my room?" I asked.

"Sure," said the bartender. "Don't worry. It's late. It's on the house."

"Thank you!"

I took off the four-inch-heel strappy sandals I'd worn all

evening and carried them in one hand, my cocktail in the other. I tiptoed up the creaky wooden staircase to the second floor. Outside my room, I saw a familiar physique with a small suitcase and garment bag trying to get into my room.

"Well, hello there. You made it, I see."

My wedding date looked up.

"Hey, are you trying to sneak up on me?" Nate asked with a smile that could melt the heart of anyone with a pulse.

I was the one who was supposed to say *surprise!*, but there he was.

"You're early," I said sarcastically.

"Sorry, I got stuck at the hospital, and the traffic was terrible. I was hoping to crash the rehearsal dinner but looks like I drove up just as everyone was leaving."

I left his name at the front desk so he could get the room key without the night clerk's having to wake me. I assumed he would arrive much later into the night. I had it all planned out. He would walk in and slip under the covers with me. Well, that's what I get for always making a plan.

"So how was your mini vacation?" he asked. Before I could answer, he filled the pause with "It would have been better with me."

"It was very nice," I said.

"Must have been really nice. Too busy to call?"

"I'll get the door."

"Let me have a sip of that," he said, nudging me with his hip.

"Are you sure you're ready for this?" I asked as I eased the key in the door.

"Ready for what?" he said, a mischievous smile on his face.

"Ha-ha. Not that. You know, ready to meet my closest friends and family?"

"Ready for that and more, Miss Jordan Manning."

• •

The wedding was as beautiful as Lisette had hoped for. And although Liz warned her bridesmaids not to cry because we'd "look terrible in the pictures," tears were unavoidable. All of us wiped away a few as she strutted regally down the wooden path resting on the sand leading her to the stunning floral arch.

The wedding party gave us all a chance to forget anything and everything in the real world. This was a good time. Weddings have a funny way of doing that. The smiles, the joy, the dancing, the love. The surprise of the evening was indeed Nate, who jumped into the electric slide formation like he had been part of the crew since college. By the time Anita Baker's "Sweet Love" whispered from the speakers, all eyes were on me and my surprise date. And yes, we gave them a show. Justice Jordan knows how to keep them guessing.

ACKNOWLEDGMENTS

Dreaming of writing this story and turning it into a book in your hands would not be possible without an army of people, all of them saying to me in their own way "you got this."

The first Jordan Manning book, *As the Wicked Watch*, was written as the world sheltered in place in 2020. I began my second book, *Watch Where They Hide*, as we refocused and reopened our individual lives post pandemic. Without Steven, my husband, I would not have been able to give energy to *Watch Where They Hide* while staying present and appreciating every moment with our son, Moses. I don't think true balance is possible, but I do believe in the feeling of doing your best. Steven, you helped me feel my best not only as a mom, but also a writer, talk show host, executive producer, and all the other titles I try to pull off.

Speaking of Moses, my "later in life" child has given me a greater balance than I could have ever imagined. Although life is no longer just about work, creating and writing the Jordan Manning series has never meant more to me. So, thank you to my two chocolate-chip-cookie-loving fellas. We had plenty of late-night cookie moments as I kept us all awake writing and taking calls discussing this book.

A sincere thank-you to a few strong and deeply passionate women who made me feel I could do it all and defy any expectations. My attorney, Bianca Levin Gang. You never ever let me down. Our eye-opening conversations about business, and even the tearful ones about motherhood, were not lost on me. AMPR Vanessa, Erin, Jordan: you ladies rock. Women betting on other women to be seen and respected will always be in style. Eve Attermann, you are a mom boss and a book boss. As a book agent you served as the champion every writer needs, especially a new one like me. I appreciate you believing in this idea from the start and working with me to make sure Jordan gets the respect and seat at the table she deserves. You were there when publishers told us how a character like Jordan is rarely seen in the thriller–true crime world. Well, she's here now because you believed in me.

Shawn Taylor—WOW!!! Thank you for your patience as I tried to do way too much all at the same time. You kept the train on the tracks and me from going off the rails. Few people have seen me on Zoom fending off a four-year-old, a puppy, deliveries from Amazon, and a chirping parrot in the background. (Shout-out to our family bird, Jojo, who tried to take over our Zooms.) Shawn, you are a wonderful soul and a true saint for putting up with the ever-changing schedule. You made certain every deadline was front of mind without compromising the story. Jordan represents so much of both of our lives as journalists hoping to do the right thing. Thank you to the team at William Morrow: Carrie Feron, Asanté Simons, and team newbie Danielle Dieterich. Danielle, you jumped in Jordan Manning–style, heart-first with a bold, hardworking spirit to match.

To my mother, Mary, who supported me from day one as I took on the new challenge of writing the Jordan Manning series. You made certain to remind me to rest, reset, and reload. That advice helped on the days I needed to dig deep to hear Jordan's voice. To my brother, Todd; my nephew, Isaiah; and my nieces, Myah, Gianna, and Laila. Each of you inspire me in unique ways. You serve as a reminder to always stay true to myself and to keep Jordan's never-give-up spirit alive in me. To my friends—if I listed your names, we would already be in book three of the series. I love y'all for sharing Jordan with everyone who would listen. The selfies in the airport bookstore of you beaming with pride are stamped in my mind. Christina, Larry, and Erika, your feedback after late-night emails helped take this story even further than I imagined. Vicky and Jenifer, thank you for holding down the fort when I needed to hide in a corner and write.

It is not lost on me how the *Tamron Hall* team shared me with the Jordan Manning universe of people without complaint. You never demanded that I stay in a box. You made it possible for me to do the show yet still have the bandwidth to take Jordan to a new level. To Bradley Singer for his support on this project and so many others. You are a truly good person—and love to your family who supported from Texas and New York City.

Thank you, Mrs. Ernestine Rose. In addition to being the high school teacher who changed my life, you are the author who continues to write about family and children with a passion that ignites a fire in me to keep creating and telling stories.

Lastly, to the Tamfam. Thank you for believing in this series and for soaking up *As the Wicked Watch* and now *Watch Where They Hide.* I was blown away every time I heard you ask about "the next Jordan Manning book." Whether on the streets, in the audience at my talk show, or in messages on social media, I heard you loud and clear.